Bound

An Evergreen Academy Novel

Ruby Vincent

Published by Ruby Vincent, 2019.

Chapter One

"**N**o!" He snapped his head to the side, almost knocking the spoon from my hand.

I sighed. "Adam, you have to eat your peas."

"No!"

Knock. Knock.

Mom dropped her amused smile long enough to get up from the table. "I'll get that."

"Come on, baby." I was reduced to pleading. "You like peas. You ate them yesterday."

The two-year-old wasn't impressed by my logic. "No!"

Refusing to give in, I inch by inch brought the baby food closer to his mouth. He watched it coming in, face wrinkled with displeasure as I touched the spoon to his—

"No!" He whipped his head the other way and the spoon popped out of my hand.

Splat!

Adam and I stared at each other as the baby food dripped down my forehead. In the next second, he was squealing with laughter.

"Val. It's for you." Grumbling, I snatched a cloth off the table and left the giggling toddler in his high chair. Mom stepped into the doorway of the dining room before I could get out. "They sure do make 'em better than they did when I went to school. If I was your age, I'd be all over that."

1

I blinked. "Over what?" Mom stepped around me and a swat landed on my backside. "Ouch!"

"Go get 'em."

Shaking my head, I stepped into the hall and my eyes fell on the people standing on my welcome mat. The towel slipped from my fingers.

"Hey, baby." Jaxson waved like it was no big deal. "Can we come in?"

I stared at him dumbfounded, brain still trying to make sense of how it was seeing Jaxson Van Zandt, Maverick Beaumont, Ezra Lennox, and Ryder Shea on my doorstep.

"Val?" A voice sounded from my bedroom. "Where is my"—Sofia stepped into the hall—"phone charger? I need— What are you guys doing here?!"

Ezra raised a brow. "Standing on the doorstep like idiots. Can we come in or not?"

Ezra followed the question by picking up his feet to come inside and I suddenly came to life. I shot forward and darted into the doorway before he could cross the threshold.

"What are you guys doing here?" My voice sounded harsh to my own ears, but I couldn't help it. I was coming off of the most intense school year of my life. After everything that happened, the five of us had limped along to the end of sophomore year not knowing how to be around each other. Now, they were here.

"We need to talk," Maverick said simply. I felt Sofia's presence over my shoulder. "Things are different now. You agree, don't you?"

"Of course, but—" I stopped, highly aware of Sofia. She didn't know what happened with Scarlett. No one did. She was our secret. "Now isn't the time."

"Now is the time." Ryder's voice pulled my eyes to him like magnets. His face was inscrutable, but there was something in his tone that brokered no argument. "Let us in."

"You'll want to hear this," Jaxson said in a more jovial tone. He had the charming smile to match. "I promise." His eyes traveled off my face and drifted down. "But first, what the fuck is on your shirt?"

I looked down and got an eyeful of the large green pea stain on my top. My cheeks flushed hot.

"I—"

"Tina! Tina! Tiiiinnnnnnnaaaaa!"

Sighing, I turned my head back toward the dining room. "My master calls," I mumbled.

"What?" Jaxson asked.

"Nothing." I stepped back and swept out my hand. "You can come in. Take off your shoes first."

The Knights filed in without another word. It was strange seeing them out of uniform. It was even stranger that somehow they still looked the same. Jaxson's laid-back, devil-may-care brand of style extended to his sagging pants and simple name-brand t-shirt. His buzz-cut days were over and now only the sides of his head were shaved while long, blond locks hung down to his ears.

Maverick always kept his coarse brown hair short. It suited him along with the jeans and tight long-sleeved shirt that wrapped around his muscles like most girls wished they could. Ezra's black hair was slicked back and perfect like his buttoned-up plaid shirt and dark jeans. Then there was Ryder.

Every time I saw Ryder Shea, I told myself there was no way he could get more gorgeous, and every time I was wrong. Ryder's raven locks had that tousled quality from running his fingers through his hair. The stud in his ear glinted in the light as he bent to remove his shoes, and fixed as I was on it, he caught my eyes the moment he turned.

Our gaze met in a spark of electricity that surged beneath my skin.

What are we now? Where do we go from—?

"Tiiinnnnaaaaa!" *Bang! Bang!* "Tina!"

Sofia chuckled. "Uh oh. You weren't quick enough and he brought out the sippy cup. I swear that kid doesn't know any other words besides 'Tina' and 'No.'"

Heaving a sigh, I hurried from the hall and burst into the entrance of the dining room. Adam's mouth was half open, readying for another scream.

"Adam!" I cried. A wide smile spread across my lips. "Adam, Adam, Adam." I hopped closer to him with every sing of his name and he grinned.

"Tina!"

"Adam!" I popped open the high chair and tackled him with tickles. The baby squealed with delight. Behind me, I could hear them moving into the room. I saw a figure walk past me out of the corner of my eye and go into the kitchen.

"Hey, kid," I heard Mom say. "Need something?"

I took Adam out of his high chair. I turned to go and bumped into a hard chest. Ryder looked down at us, or I should say, he looked down at my son.

"This is Adam."

I held the baby a little tighter. "Yes."

What is he thinking? Looking down at the kid who could rip his entire fortune away from him and leave him and his mother with nothing.

Ryder lifted his hands. "Can I hold him?"

I blinked. I wasn't ready for that. "I don't know if that's a—"

My stranger-loving son opened up his arms and fell into Ryder's hands. Ryder settled the baby against his chest and gazed at him with an emotion I couldn't read, and I was studying his every blink and twitch. Adam seemed to be doing the same, scrunching up his little nose as he looked at the new person.

Jaxson, Maverick, and Sofia watched the exchange from their seats at the dining table. I could feel the tension coming off of Sofia because it mirrored my own. She knew who Adam's father was, and she knew Ryder did too.

Ryder finally spoke. "He's cute. Looks like you."

"Yes... he does." Adam truly did look like me. He had my green eyes, brown curls, and according to Mom, my smile. There was no trace of Benjamin Shea in his tiny face.

"Hmm."

Ryder turned to go.

"Where are you going?" I quickly darted in front of him, hands already up for my son.

"I'm going to sit down."

"B-but I should take him." I took Adam's arm. "Come to Tina, baby."

Adam's response was to rest his head on Ryder's shoulder, getting comfortable. Above him, Ryder smirked at me. A smirk I hadn't seen for a while.

"What do you think I'm going to do, Moon?"

I pressed my lips together. I was not hiding my anxiety well.

"He's in good hands. Trust me."

Ryder stepped around me for the living room, and I was right behind him. "Ryd—"

"You did what?!"

The shout brought me to a jerking halt.

"I can't apologize enough for— Ow! Ow, ow, ow!"

"You've got some balls, kid! What were you trying to do?!"

I spun around and tore into the dining room. The three of them at the table stared with wide eyes into the kitchen where my mother had Ezra Lennox, son of the queen of media, by the ear.

Ezra was bright red in her grasp. "I'm sorry! I'm sorry! I know it was wrong!"

"Where do you get off showing videos of me?! Were you trying to mess with my daughter?!"

My mouth fell open. *Video? Did Ezra tell her about freshman year and the Parents' Day clip? Why?*

"I was," he cried. "It wasn't right and I'll make it up to her too."

Mom growled. "You're not done making it up to me. Let's go."

I stood rooted to the spot as Olivia dragged Ezra out. The front door slammed on his pleas.

Jaxson's fingers drummed on the table. "Is she going to kill him?"

I shook my head. "I honestly don't know."

"Well, it'd be a shame if she took him down on the first one. He's got two more to go."

"What?" I asked, a bit absentmindedly. My attention was on Ryder and Adam. My body itched to follow them into the living room.

"That's what we came to talk to you about."

"What is?" I edged out of the room.

"Have you ever heard of—"

"Excuse me a sec." Cutting off Jaxson midstream, I hurried out and practically ran for the living room.

Why are they so quiet? What is going—

"—magical forest. The trees sang and the grass remembered those who passed over their heads."

I gaped at the sight. Ryder sat on our couch reading Adam his favorite book. The two-year-old rested contentedly on his chest, eyelids rising and falling as he fought sleep.

"You don't have to do that," I said softly. I think I meant that more than one way.

Ryder lifted his gaze. "I know. I want to." I think he meant that more than one way too.

Despite myself, I swallowed the protests that fought to leave my lips. Instead, I moved closer to them and took a seat by his side. Our connection didn't break as I brushed against his arm, but for a second, his face changed. An odd look overcame him, morphing a blank expression into a mask of intensity.

"Valentina—"

"What's this about you coming up for the summer?" Jaxson strolled into the living room with Maverick and Sofia on his heels. "Sofi says you're staying with her?"

"She is," Sofia confirmed. She came over and wedged herself between me and the arm of the couch. "I stayed with her while my parents were in Thailand. They're back now and have ordered me home. I agreed as long as Val could come with."

"Sweet. You'll be close by."

I made a face. "Close by for what?"

Jaxson grinned as he sat down in the armchair across from me. "Have you ever heard of the Twelve Labors of Hercules?"

"I heard too much about it from Wheeldon. What's it got to do with anything?"

"Here's the thing." Jaxson leaned forward, propping his elbows on his knees. "We've been assholes—"

"No arguments here."

"—but we're done with that." He went on like there was no interruption. "The mark and the stuff we pulled; we never wanted to do it anyway. Things got crazy last year and I think all of us are sick of it." Jaxson glanced around and was met with Maverick's—and Ryder's—nod.

I looked at the three of them with wide eyes. *What was going on here?*

"Now that we don't have to worry about the Spades; we don't have to keep on with the bull"—he cut eyes to Adam—"crap," Jaxson finished.

Maverick stepped forward. "We know we have a lot to make up for with you, and breaking our stuff and leaking songs doesn't cover it. We want to apologize for real."

I looked between the two of them, mouth hanging open. "I'm sorry. Is this seriously happening?"

Jaxson swept out his hands. "We're calling it the Twelve Labors of the Knights."

"We're not calling it that." Ryder's dry voice broke through my haze. "It's simple, Val. We want to do something to get you to forgive us."

"Three somethings," Jaxson explained. "Three each for four of us so twelve." He jerked his thumb over his shoulder. "And Ezra kicked it off by fessing up to your mom what he did with the spring break video. We all have something planned for you... if you'll let us."

My eyes traced over their faces, considering. I didn't know what to make of this. The last few weeks of sophomore year we had been civil to each other, but there had been no talk of apologies. Now this?

I took a deep breath. "I deserve an apology after what you all put me through, so fine. I'll go along."

Jaxson nodded. "Good. Just one more thing."

I waited.

"About my three." He cocked his head. "Does hooking up in the bathroom count as one because I feel like we made a lot of progress that day."

Cheeks flaming, I seized a pillow quicker than he could blink and lobbed it at him. It nailed him head-on and he guffawed. "Take that as a no. It's cool, baby. I'll get even more creative for the rest."

I did not miss the note of suggestion in that reply. A flush crept up my neck as I remembered my spur-of-the-moment, hot-off-a-win kiss with Jaxson after the hip-hop contest. That was another thing we hadn't talked about after Scarlett's fall.

"Give me the phone!"

The memory lashed across my mind, chasing thoughts of the kiss away. My hands clenched into fists as my heart sped up. I never thought I would be responsible for the loss of a life, let alone two. No one could know what truly happened to Scarlett LeBlanc, the Evergreen art teacher who up and disappeared after leaving a simple resignation letter on her desk.

I wish I didn't know. I wish her screams hadn't joined the chorus of shrieks in my dreams.

"Adam?" I shook myself back to reality as Ryder looked down at the toddler. "The kid is out."

"I'll take him." I rose and Ryder passed the sleeping baby into my hands. "I'll get him down and then finish packing."

"I'll help." Sofia got up and trailed me to my room. She pounced on me the moment she closed the door. "Val, what do you think? Do you trust them?"

I placed Adam on my bed and pulled the covers to his chin. "I guess I have to."

"Does this mean you're friends now? Are you dating Jaxson?"

I tossed my head. "I can't even begin to think about what this means. First, let's see if they can apologize to me as well as they torture me."

"Oh, Val." She looked so worried I wanted to say something to reassure her, but I had no clue what.

"Let's just pack. We have a month of summer left and we're going to spend it soaking up the sun by the pool and shopping till our bank accounts cry."

She cracked a smile. "But first, your seventeenth birthday party."

"Do not say party. *No* parties. I just want to hang out, grab dinner, and maybe catch a movie."

Sofia rolled her eyes. "Come on. It won't be like last time."

"You mean when you dropped an entire cake on my head or having my class whisper diseased slut at me all night? The Knights already know we're friends, but the rest of the school doesn't. We have to keep it that way."

Groaning, she replied, "Fine. One incredibly boring seventeenth birthday celebration coming up."

"That's the spirit."

We hurried to finish packing the rest of our things. The car Madeline sent would be here any minute.

I paused in stuffing a handful of underwear in my duffle and looked at Adam. "I wish he could come with us."

Sofia glanced up from putting away her makeup. "Me too, but Mom was clear on not surprising her with any more babies. Besides, it's only for a few weeks and we can drive down to see him whenever you want." She beamed. "In my new car."

I tried for a smile, but I knew it was sad around the edges. "Can't wait to see your car. You've only been talking about it like it's *your* baby since you got here."

She laughed. "It might as well be. I love that thing. If Mom hadn't forbidden me from driving while she was out of town and stole my keys, I'd be with it now." She tossed the makeup in her bag and reached for her clothes. "Are you getting a car?"

I scoffed. "And go where? From my dorm to the sports complex? Evergreen keeps us locked up tighter than convicts."

"Can't argue with that. I won't lie; I'm not looking forward to going back to school this year. The collective weight of the donors' displeasure may have gotten Evergreen to back off the no-phone ban, but the guy's still a tyrant. Who knows what he'll come up with next?"

"It shouldn't be so bad."

"Hmm. Famous last words?"

"Sofia!"

Cackling, Sofia gathered her stuff and headed for the door. I made sure to kiss Adam's soft cheek before following her out. "Bye, son. I love you."

Ryder, Maverick, and Jaxson stood in the hallway when we came out. "Ready?" Jaxson asked. "Both cars are out front."

"I'm ready."

The five of us stepped through the door in time to see a red-faced Ezra push the lawnmower from the garage. Mom planted herself in the driveway, hands on hips. "And when you're done with that, I've got gutters for you to clean out and dishes for you to wash."

Ezra looked from us to her, almost pleading. "But we're leaving."

Her eyes sharpened. "You're not."

"But—"

Jaxson tossed his friend a salute. "See ya, playboy. We'll send the car back for you."

"Jaxson!"

The Knights turned their back on him and tromped to their waiting limo. I almost felt bad for him—almost.

"Bye, Olivia." I ran up and gave her a hug. "I'll see you next week for my birthday."

"Of course, kid." Mom's sweet tone was night and day from the one she had reserved for Ezra. "We'll both be there. You have fun with Sofia." She dropped a kiss on my head. "And don't worry; I'll make sure this guy learns the meaning of respect."

Laughing, I tossed Ezra a wink from the circle of her arms. "I know you will. Love you."

"Love you, too."

I waved over my shoulder as I headed for the second limo. I could feel the eyes peeking through the windows at the sleek black rides taking up the street. I didn't know our neighbors very well, but after this, they were probably thinking they needed to get to know me.

I slid in beside Sofia as she took to chattering about what we were going to do for the next few weeks.

"Twelve Labors of the Knights."

Things were definitely going to be interesting.

Chapter Two

"Valerie, darling." Madeline enfolded me in a cloud of cashmere and rose perfume. "It's wonderful to see you."

"It's Valentina, Mom." Sofia slipped her bag off her shoulder and her staff was at her side in a second to take it off her hands.

The Richards Estate was as spectacular as I remembered—rolling hills, manicured gardens, and three stories of wealth and elegance contained within a Georgian-style home.

Standing at Madeline's side was a slightly balding man with silver-framed glasses that I had never met before. He inclined his head at me in greeting.

"Hello, girls."

"Hi, Daddy." Sofia launched herself at him. He laughed, spinning her off her feet.

"How is my favorite daughter?"

"Your only daughter," she shot back, "unless you have something to tell me."

"Shh." His eyes widened. "Not in front of your mother."

They cracked up while Madeline's lips pursed.

"Honestly, you two. We have a guest." She snapped her fingers and one of the staff sprang forward to take my things. "Come, Valentina. We have so much planned for your stay and we can't waste a moment." She seized me and drew me to her side. "Your birthday is next week and there is much to do."

"Wait," I cut in, stiffening. "Not another birthday party."

"No." Madeline looked across to Sofia. Lines appeared on her face to show off her disapproval. "Sofia said if I tried, she'd throw another cake on you. I don't know what's gotten into that girl."

Sofia and I looked at each other and tried not to bust a gut. I didn't know about her methods, but my bestie got things done.

"It'll be a simple dinner with our families and then presents, but leading up to it will be shopping, manicures, pedicures, and what do you think about another haircut? The bob really suited you. Or how about—"

"Let's not overwhelm her on the first day, dear." Sofia's dad placed her back on her feet and reached out to shake my hand. "My name is Oliver Richards. I've heard a lot about you, Valentina. We're excited to have you staying with us."

As for me, I had heard very little about Oliver Richards and Sofia and I had been friends for two years. One surprise being that the guy had an English accent.

"Thank you."

"Well, let's not hang about on the doorstep. We had the cook make all your favorites. Get settled in and then we'll have dinner."

"Sounds good."

Sofia grabbed my arm and led me inside ahead of her parents. "I swear we will have fun in between Mom's makeover attempts. Dad likes to go big to make up for being away all the time so whatever we ask, he'll do. I'm serious. Have you ever wanted to go to Venice? 'Cause he'd book the tickets tomorrow."

"I know we'll have fun," I said between chuckling. "But don't let me get in the way of you spending time with your parents."

"Oh, please. You're not in the way. You basically are family."

I ducked my head. I didn't let on how much that meant to me, but I figured Sofia knew me well enough to know how much it did. Everything I had gone through at Evergreen; I was glad I hadn't lost her. I could face anything as long as I had her, including whatever our junior year would bring.

"VAL!" THE CRY WENT with a pounding on my door.

"Come—"

Sofia already threw it open.

"—in."

She flopped down on my bed and burrowed into my side as I set the laptop on the bedside table.

"What are you doing?"

"Signing up for classes." I flapped a hand at the screen. "Our schedule is brutal this year. Plus, did you see that classes aren't split anymore?"

"Yeah, it happens when too many people wash out. Things got so crazy with people being expelled and pulled out after the Evergreen Gone Wild video, and then finals were so brutal. We're all in the same classes now which means..."

"Natalie, Airi, Isabella, and everyone who made my life hell will be sitting a couple rows over for the entire year," I finished. "Fun."

"At least we'll be in the same class again."

"Along with Paisley, Eric, and Claire. Eric didn't mess with me while we were on the dance team, but he made it clear we weren't friends."

"Eric takes the school's traditions seriously. He comes after two generations of Knights." She picked her head up and gave me a look. "Speaking of Eric... he wants to hang out tonight. Last time, he got super suspicious when I kept dodging him, but if you don't want me to go," she added quickly, "I won't. Tomorrow is your birthday and we can spend the night binge-watching and sneaking Madame Madeline's cookies from her hiding spot."

"Tempting, but that's okay." I bumped her shoulder. "It's cool with me that you're still friends. You don't have to feel bad for hanging out with him."

"Are you sure?"

"I'm sure. Go ahead."

She beamed. "You're the best." The next thing I knew she was grabbing my arm and hauling me up. "You can help me pick out an outfit. I'm meeting up with Eric and his boyfriend, and he says they're bringing a *friend*. It's so obvious he's setting me up, but your girl hasn't had sex for like six months so I'm not complaining."

I laughed. "Does he go to Evergreen?"

"Yes." Sofia was practically skipping down the hall to her room. "He's new. He's transferring in this year from—get this—South Africa. You know their accents are wicked sexy."

"This I do know."

We went into her room and I could see an attempt had been made to find her outfit already. Clothes were strewn all over the place and I had to shove a pile of dresses out of the way to sit on the edge of her mattress.

Sofia disappeared into her walk-in closet. Her voice floated out of the doors. "You remember the girl that tried to cheat to beat Cade out for top of the class?"

"Yeah. What about her?"

"That was Su Hee Kim. The Kims moved out of Evergreen after she was expelled and his family moved into their mansion. He lives like ten minutes away."

"Convenient if he does become your new hookup."

"Exactly." Sofia poked her head out and gave me a wink. "This is why you're my best friend. You get me."

The rest of her moved into sight and she showed off her outfit. "What do you think?"

Sofia had gone for a sheer white dress with a white slip underneath. It was cute, but—

"We can do better than that. What about that red top with your black skirt?"

"Ohh!" She darted away and was gone again. "Eric also said he has a twin, but he's not coming tonight."

"What are you guys going to do?"

"We're watching a movie in his private theater, then I'm taking my baby out and we're showing him around town." With a leap, she was back in the entrance. "Is this the one?"

"Oh, yes, that's the one. You. Look. Hot."

She giggled. "Thank you. Thank you." Her top didn't show any cleavage, but it clung to her dips and curves in all the right ways. It went perfectly with the ruffled skirt and long, milky legs that flowed out of it. "I wish you could come with us."

I laughed. "Why would you want me there while you're trying to get some?"

"You know what I mean." Sofia came out and sat next to me. "I wish we could all be friends again like we were before you were marked. I know Paisley misses you even though she won't say it, and Claire thinks all of this is stupid."

"That didn't stop both of them from joining in. Claire and I knew each other before I ever came here and she was quick to call me a whore and say I was chasing after the daddy that ran out on me. How do we go back after that?"

"I was awful to you too." Shame laced Sofia's voice. "But we're still friends."

"You turned your back on the Knights, the Spades, all of it and stood by me. You've proved a hundred times over you're my friend. They haven't even tried."

She said nothing, just rested her head on my shoulder.

I don't know how long we sat there, but we were jarred back to the moment when her phone went off. Sofia plucked it off the nightstand.

"Hey, Eric. I'll meet you guys there in twenty minutes. Caramel popcorn. You bring that lightly salted, no-butter shit near me I'm kicking you out of your own house. I know, but we're looking at another year of Evergreen's insane diet. Caramel popcorn. Okay, fine. See you."

Turning to me, Sofia hung up. "Eric's dad had a heart attack and now the whole house is on a heart-healthy diet."

My eyes widened. "What? Is he okay?"

"He's fine. He's even back at work, but his mom is real serious about no junk food in the house. I've got to go out and get my own popcorn. Want to come? I'll drop you back."

I shrugged. "Sure. Why not?"

I was dressed in sweats and an old tank top, but there wasn't any need to get fancy for a trip to the grocery store. I twisted my hair in a messy ponytail and we headed out.

"I hope this guy is as cute as Eric says he is." Sofia grabbed her keys out of her purse and reached for the door handle. "'Cause if I can get there before the horde of Evergreen girls descend, I'm not passing that up."

"Be honest." I flicked her shoulder. "You were going tonight whether I said I was okay with it or not."

Sofia lifted her nose in the air. "As your best friend, I will not answer that."

Laughing, we threw open the door and burst out—

—running right into Jaxson Van Zandt.

"Whoa." Jaxson caught me before I could go down. His arms encircled my waist and pulled me close. "Careful, baby. Don't break yourself before we go out."

"Jaxson?" I twisted in his hold until we were face to face, my chest pressed against his. "What are you doing here?"

"Ezra had his turn and now it's mine. I've got a lot of making up to do, so we'll leave whenever you're ready. Although..." Jaxson looked down into the ample cleavage my tank top was displaying. "I like what you've got on."

I scrambled out of his arms. "Where do you think you're taking me?"

"It's a surprise, but trust me, you'll like it." Jaxson looked plenty sure of himself, grinning away like there was a prize at the end of this.

I hesitated as I glanced over his shoulder. A Rolls-Royce sat in Sofia's driveway and next to it was a blank-faced driver waiting to chauffeur us around. This was like something out of a movie, but in none of the rom-coms I've seen did the guy and girl have a history like we did. "Jaxson... I don't know."

His smile softened, morphing from smug to one that bordered on sweet. "This is for you, Val. For your birthday. I know you'll love it." He reached up and brushed the hair behind my ear, stroking my cheek as he pulled back.

It was hard to say no to Jaxson when he turned on the charm. It was even harder when he did that.

"Okay," I said softly. "Give me a minute and I'll change. Bye, Sofia."

"See you. Have fun."

I ran back inside. My duffle was torn apart as I searched for anything remotely decent to wear on a—

On a what? A date? The thought froze me stiff. *Was this a date?*

"Darling?"

I jerked toward the door. "Wha—Yes, Madeline?"

"There is a handsome boy downstairs waiting for you," she said through the wood. "Are you ready?"

"Almost." Not knowing what else to wear, I grabbed a simple, black jersey dress off the pile and shed my clothes. I was always packing accessories so I donned my diamond earrings and necklace while I shoved my feet into a cute pair of embroidered flats.

I did a spin before the vanity. I looked good. Effortlessly good, like I wasn't treating this as a date, but I still had to look hot.

Jaxson was waiting for me at the front door when I returned. He held it open before following me out. Jaxson climbed into the car without a word to the driver. Everyone knew where we were going but me.

"Can I get a hint?" I asked.

"Nope." Jaxson took my hand and laced our fingers together. That was it. No warning. No asking. He held my hand like it was the most natural thing in the world, while I prayed my palms didn't get sweaty.

"Is it far?" Nerves tickled my throat and made it croak. I took a steadying breath and tried not to think about how good it felt with him stroking the back of my hand.

"It's not too far. Twenty minutes."

I waited for him to say more, but nothing came.

"Do we have to sit in silence for this surprise? Talk to me."

Jaxson laughed. "Sorry, mama. Guess I'm afraid if I talk, I'll give it away. Tell me about your summer."

"It was good," I replied, slightly mollified. "Sofia stayed over and Mom surprised us with a trip to the beach last weekend. I've only ever been a couple of times."

"We can change that."

"You offering to take me to the beach?"

"Am I offering to get you dripping wet and sandy in a bikini? Um, yes."

"Jaxson!" I whacked his shoulder while he guffawed. "You know, you don't have to say exactly what you're thinking all the time."

"Why not?" His eyes danced as he draped his arm over my shoulder and drew me close. "You like that about me."

I could have denied it, but the truth was I did. I've never dealt with anyone so up-front and it was refreshing.

"How was your summer?" I asked.

"Not bad. Papa Van Zandt forgave me halfway through and released me from lockdown."

"It must have helped that none of the artists sued the label in the end." I had been following the Interstellar Records story like a hawk. I didn't regret what I did to get back at Jaxson, but getting the label in trouble wasn't my intention. I breathed a huge sigh of relief when no one pressed charges.

"That's true," he added. "Anyway, he's been stressed so we took a quick trip to the Bahamas. It was cool."

I was glad Jaxson couldn't see my eye roll. If I had been lucky enough to go to the Bahamas, I would have more to say than it was cool.

We talked a bit more about our summers as the car zipped through the streets. I was so engrossed in our conversation it was a while before I looked out the window and noticed we weren't in Evergreen anymore.

"Where are we?"

"Cottonwood. The next town over."

I slipped out of his hold and scooted closer to the window. Cottonwood was near our little patch of crazy, but it wasn't the same. This town had smaller homes, but bigger shopping centers with more bargains than designer labels. Some of the students who went to Evergreen on scholarship were from here.

My face was pressed to the glass when I finally saw it. I gasped. "Jaxson, no way."

"Way. Thought you'd like to see how it's all done."

The breath left my lungs as the sign for Interstellar Records loomed before us. It was a massive building that took up almost the whole block. The car stopped before the gate and a guard leaned out of the box while I tried to contain my excitement. If I wasn't careful, I would end up kissing him.

"Jaxson, this is amazing!" I burst out. "What are we going to do? Who are we going to see? Will we get to listen in? Can we—"

"Slow down, mama. We can't listen to anyone after what I pulled, but I can still take you around and sneak you into one of the studios. I'll show you how they make music magic."

"I'll take it." I bounced on the seat, grinning from ear to ear. "I'd be skipping if all you showed me was the bathroom."

The gates rumbled open for the car to pull in. The driver dropped us off at the door and Jaxson had to rush to catch up with me since I raced out of the car the second it stopped. He managed to get to the door before I did and held it open for me to go inside.

The inside of Interstellar was even more amazing than I imagined. There were black marble floors with flecks of white that made it look like an endless night sky. On the walls were photos of some of the artists that had worked with the label over the years. Almost all of them were artists I loved.

"Jaxson, this is incredible," I breathed. There was no one about, signaling business hours were over, but just being here was enough.

"And you haven't seen the best part yet." Jaxson's hand brushed the back of mine. It was me who turned my palm and linked our fingers together.

He led me off through the lobby and gave me the tour. My mouth hung open the entire time, awed by the place that had been his second home. He took me into one of the recording studios and patiently explained what every knob, button, and switch did. In the end, he had to pull me away to show me the rest.

"There's one more thing I want to show you," he said, laughing. "On the top floor."

We rode the elevator up and stepped out into a reception area. Couches lined the opposite wall, and in front of us was a single desk sitting empty.

"This is Dad's office," he explained.

"Won't we get in trouble for being in here?"

"I won't tell if you don't."

Maybe I should have fought harder, but who was I kidding? I wanted to see inside that office more than anything.

Jaxson and I passed the reception desk for a short hallway. The double doors at the end read one name: Levi Van Zandt.

He took a key out of his pocket and unlocked it. Stepping aside, he let me go in first.

"Wow," I breathed.

There were more photos of famous people in here, but this time, Levi stood in those shots right along with them. His *office* was more like a penthouse studio apartment. He had a minibar, couches, television, massive black rug taking up most of the space, and a desk where a bed would have been if this was an apartment. Then of course, there was the best part of all.

"Jaxson, what am I looking at?" My legs carried me closer even though my eyes were having trouble comprehending that this was real.

"You're looking at one of the largest record collections in the state."

The entire back wall behind Levi's desk was rows and rows of shelving, all stuffed with records. I had always thought of starting a record collection when I was out of school and living in the home I had bought for me, Mom, and Adam. If it was even a fifth of this, I would be ecstatic.

"Go ahead." I turned to Jaxson as he took a seat on the couch. "Check them out."

"I thought records were off-limits?"

He grinned. "Mine are. Dad's records are fair game."

I wasn't about to argue any more lest he changed his mind. I skirted around the desk and laid my hands on the first record I saw.

"The Black Keys. Blur. Boards of Canada!" I whipped around, clutching the album. "People think I'm all about hip-hop, but I love all kinds of music—new and old. I love the way it sucks you in."

"How it makes you feel."

"That you can forget about the world for just those few minutes."

"That a song says what you're thinking better than you ever could."

I brought the record to my lips, hiding my smile. We were so on the same wavelength right now it was incredible. "Exactly."

Jaxson stood. "Pick one and we'll play it."

"Seriously?"

"Of course."

"Okay." I was so giddy I was bouncing on my heels. I took my time searching through the shelves until my eyes lit on the perfect one "How about this one?" I held up *Bob Marley and the Wailers*. "My neighbor used to play all of his songs when she babysat me. She'd sing at the top of her lungs while I danced around the living room."

Jaxson cracked a smile as he took it from me. "My mom did too. I remember standing on her feet while we danced to his tracks. Dad would just watch. The man can't dance for shit."

I giggled. We reached for each other's hands at the same time as we moved over to the record player. Soon the magnificent space was filled with Bob Marley's voice and I swayed as it took me over.

"Dance with me?"

Jaxson gathered me in his arms before I had a chance to reply, but it didn't occur to me to say no. I draped my arms around his neck and let him mold our bodies together. The first time I danced with Jaxson I marveled at how in tune we were. This time was no different. Eyes locked, we danced as one. When I stepped, he stepped. When I moved, he moved with me.

As the song shifted into another, Jaxson rested his forehead against mine. His hair tickled me and without thinking I reached up to push it back. He turned and pressed a kiss to my palm before

I could pull away. The act made my pulse quicken beneath the ghost mark of his lips.

Jaxson turned back to me, eyes aflame with heat, and I was starkly reminded of that day in the bathroom clinging to him while he enticed moan after moan from my lips.

He smiled. "You're blushing. What are you thinking about?"

My cheeks grew hotter. "Nothing."

"Are you thinking about me kissing you? Because I promise I'm thinking about the same thing."

"I might be," I whispered, "but I'm also thinking..."

Jaxson drew me closer if such a thing were possible. We were already as close as two people could be. "What's wrong, baby?"

I bit my lip hard. "You're not... going to hurt me again, are you?"

He stopped dead. "What? Val, no. Never again."

"How do I know that's true?"

"Because I— Argh." Stepping back, he dropped his arms. I missed the loss for the barest moment until he cupped my face in his hands. "Because I always wanted you. From the beginning, Val. From the moment I heard of the beautiful new girl who blew in to shake things up. I wanted *you*."

"But that's not true," I cried. I tugged at his hands. "I was a stupid bet between you and the Knights. Who could get in my pants first? None of it was real. You— Why are you shaking your head?!"

"Don't you get it?" He gave me a little shake. "There was no bet. There was *never* a bet."

"But you said—"

"We said that because you were marked. We wanted to hurt you, Val, and what better way than thinking the guys who liked you were playing you all along."

I made a choked noise, gaping at him in shock. "Well, congratulations. It did fucking hurt!"

"And I'm sorry. You'll never know how sorry I am." Jaxson's eyes were shimmering pools of blue. They pulled me in, and then pulled me under. "I don't owe you three apologies; I owe you thousands. You're smart and beautiful and strong, and I tried to break you on the card of a monster."

"Jaxson."

"I know I don't deserve you, but I want you anyway."

"Jaxson."

"I'll take whatever part of you that you'll give me. I—"

I pressed my fingers to his mouth. "Jaxson, stop talking and kiss me."

He blinked. "What?"

"Kiss me."

His expression changed. In the next breath, my finger was gone and replaced by my lips. The kiss was reminiscent of the one we shared in the bathroom—all heat and fire and passion, but this time there was something more. Something that rode the wave of our intensity and filled me as fast as my need for him.

It felt like... forgiveness. I had let go, and let Jaxson in.

His hands moved to my thighs and suddenly I was up. I laughed into the kiss as he carried me over to the couch and set me down. I tugged at the hem of his shirt. Jaxson stepped back long enough to rip it over his head and then his mouth was on mine again.

The nerves beneath my skin tingled and sizzled like things that had just come alive. I might have floated away if my entire being wasn't anchored to Jaxson and this kiss. I sank down onto the couch, bringing him with me.

We broke apart as Jaxson nipped a path to my neck. He found the spot he discovered last time and licked, eliciting a gasp.

"Jaxson," I breathed.

"Yes, baby?" Another lick and I arched my back. He was driving me crazy and he hadn't even gotten to the interesting parts.

"I... need you to go slow, okay?"

He lifted his head to meet my eyes. "Val, of course. We won't do anything that you don't want to do. If you want to stop—"

"No." Biting my lip, I took a steadying breath to get the rest out. "That's not what I'm saying. I want to. I want *you*. Here. Now. I just... need you to take it slowly. This is new for me."

"Okay." He bent and gave me a soft peck on the lips. "Slow it is."

He kissed me again, softly this time, while his hands traveled down my body and then under my dress. He slid it up over my thighs, then my waist, then my stomach, then my breasts. His movements were so excruciatingly languid I almost told him to drop the slow stuff right there.

It's okay, Val. You have all night. It's just you and Jaxson.

My dress fell to the floor and Jaxson's pants quickly followed. My hands explored his body like it was a wonderland. I loved the feel of him beneath my palm—hard, strong, but also warm.

Jaxson broke our kiss and pressed his mouth to my shoulder. With his teeth, he slid the bra strap down until my breast sprang free. His chest rose and fell beneath my hands as he panted.

"Can I?"

I nodded, not trusting myself to speak. He bent his head.

Ring! Ring!

Jaxson's head snapped up. "You got to be fucking kidding me right now!"

I giggled. "It's okay. I'm not going anywhere. Just turn it off."

Cursing, Jaxson fumbled to get his phone out of his pants. "There. Now— Fuck!"

"What's wrong?"

"Son." I froze as a dry voice sounded in my ears. "I wouldn't hang up if I were you."

Jaxson looked so wretched I might have laughed. The poor guy had accidentally accepted the call.

He sighed. "Yes, Dad?"

"I know you're at the studio," Levi said, "and I know you're with a girl."

"What?" I hissed. I yanked my bra on like we were being watched.

"How do you— Wait. Clive ratted me out, didn't he? The overpaid bastard."

Levi actually chuckled. "The overpaid bastard is overpaid by me. He knows better than to lie to me when I ask where my son is. He told me he's waiting outside for you and a charming young lady so you're going to stop what you're doing, put everything back where you found it, and get in the car. If Clive doesn't call me back in five minutes to say you're walking out of the door, you're spending the next month in your room."

"Alright, Pops. We're leaving."

"Thank you. See you home in an hour."

Click.

Jaxson hung his head, resting it on my chest. "I love that guy, but he's got the worst timing."

I poked him. "Speaking of timing. We should go before you get grounded."

With obvious reluctance, we clambered off the couch, got dressed, and did as his father instructed. It was only when we were in the car zooming out of Cottonwood did it hit me that I had been about to have sex with Jaxson. It was insane how much I had wanted him at that moment—how much I still wanted him.

He placed his hand on mine. "Hope I did good for my first labor."

"It was perfect. I can't wait to see what you have in mind for number two and three."

He gazed at me steadily. "There won't be any interruptions next time."

I shivered under the look in his eyes. "I hope so."

Jaxson pulled me to his side and I burrowed into his warmth. We sat there quiet and content until Sofia's mansion came into view.

"There's one more thing," he began. "We're going to Ryder's place on Sunday. There's a lot of things we need to talk about now that school is starting again. We thought you should be there."

I tilted my head back. "Really? Is this about last semester?"

He nodded.

"Then I'll be there."

"Nice. I'll send a car for you."

We didn't speak any more about it. Jaxson and I shared one last kiss before Clive opened the door.

I escaped up to my room, showered, and hopped into bed with every intention of going to sleep, but thoughts of Jaxson and me on that couch plagued my mind.

"Val?"

Knock. Knock.

"Val, you awake?"

I glanced at the clock as I pushed myself up. It was after midnight. "I'm up. Come in."

Sofia eased open the door. Her shadowed figure crept closer to the bed until I felt it dip. She settled down next to me.

During the day, she busted in and out as she pleased, but at night she was understanding about giving me warning before approaching me in the dark.

"Did you have fun tonight?" I asked.

She tittered. "So much fun. Zane is smoking hot, Val. I almost jumped him the second I saw him."

"Did you guys hit it off?"

"I'd say so." The suggestion in her voice was so heavy only an idiot could have mistaken it.

"So. Fi. A!" I cried. "You hooked up with him, didn't you?"

"Only a little."

"How do you hook up with a guy a little?"

"We made out during the movie, that's it. But he did invite me to his place on Sunday after your birthday. Will you be okay if I go? I'm cool to hang with you instead."

I blew a raspberry on that. "Forget about me. You're working on a summer romance, don't let me stand in the way. Besides, I've got somewhere to be on Sunday too."

"Great. So what did you and Jaxson do tonight?"

"We went to his dad's record label. It was amazing. He gave me a tour and we listened to records and..." I trailed off, preparing myself for what was coming next. "Don't freak, okay."

I felt her shift. "Freak about what?"

"Jaxson and I hooked up too."

"What?!"

"And we almost had sex."

"What?!"

I bounced as she suddenly jerked up. Before I knew it, light was flooding my eyes. Sofia flicked on the lamp and turned it on me.

"Sofia, I told you not to freak."

"Screw that. Tell me everything."

I heaved a sigh, but inside I was fighting a smile. It's not like I didn't know this was coming. I scrambled up and propped myself against the pillows. "Okay, so we were dancing and..."

IT WAS A SLEEP-DEPRIVED wreck that answered the door the next morning.

"Tina!"

I immediately perked up at the sight of my son. We weren't apart long and I had missed him like crazy. "Hi, baby." I held out my arms and he fell into them. Mom followed behind with a hug.

"How's my seventeen-year-old?"

"I'm good." I kissed Adam's curls. "And better now that you're here. But you didn't have to come so early. Madeline is taking us out to dinner at six."

"I know. That's why I wanted time with you first. Just the three of us on your birthday. Sound good?"

"Love that."

I gave them a brief tour of the place and then we were out. It was perfect getting to spend the day talking, shopping, and playing with Adam. It was exactly what I wanted for my birthday. As the clock neared six, Sofia walked into my room to find Mom and me wearing the dresses we bought at the promenade. I was in the middle of getting Adam into his suit. It was taking a while because I couldn't resist stopping every five seconds to take pictures.

"Sofia, you look great." The pink tea-length dress she chose showcased all of her best features—not that she had any bad ones.

"Thanks. You do too." She lifted her hand and I noticed the small present hanging off her finger. "Is now a good time to give you your gift?"

"Sure."

Mom scooped up Adam. "I will finish getting him dressed. We'll see you downstairs."

Sofia handed it over after the door closed behind them. "Open it."

I reached inside and took out the small, rectangular box. Nestled inside was a gorgeous gold bracelet.

"Sofia, thank you."

"I have one too." She took the box from me. "It's not the same color or style, but I put the same engraving on the back so we never forget how we became friends." She lifted the band and held it out to me. "Read it."

I took one look at it and burst out laughing. "Strawberry root beer." Eyes prickling, I grabbed her in a hug. "I love it so much."

Soon we sucked up the tears and headed downstairs. Everyone was waiting for us at the door.

"Wow, we look good," I teased. "Where we are going, we're about to make those fire alarms go wild."

Madeline threw her head back laughing. "You're such a scream, darling. Come, come. We don't want to miss our reservations."

The restaurant Sofia's parents booked was high-end in the extreme. Mom and I bought gowns for the celebration and we still felt underdressed. Even so, I had a great time. We laughed, joked, and stuffed ourselves on the tastiest food I had ever eaten. Adam delighted everyone with his cuteness, and by the end of the night, not even Madeline could resist holding him.

Mom and Adam spent the night after we stumbled back to the mansion. They squeezed in with me despite the Richards offering up their fifty-odd spare bedrooms. I snuggled up with my baby and fell asleep feeling so happy I could bust. I knew her screams wouldn't find my dreams when sleep claimed me.

"BYE, MOM. I'LL COME back at the end of summer."

"You better. It's our ritual for me to do this awful drive and drop you at those gates. No reason to stop now."

"Agreed." I gave them both one more kiss and hug.

Mom honked her way down the massive driveway as I waved. When they were gone, I made to go back inside.

Buzz. Buzz.

I answered my phone without looking at the screen. "Hello?"

"Try that again and you're going down, playboy— Hey!"

There was a shout, the obvious sound of fighting, and then laughter that faded as cursing took its place.

"People think Ricky is nice," Jaxson raged. "Asshole! Motherfu—" There was a bang. "No throwing!"

I stifled a laugh. "What the hell are you guys doing?"

"Minding my own business watching a movie," he grumbled. "Then the big guy decides he wants to watch some stupid gadget show and attacks. There are six other televisions in this house!"

Maverick's shout came through clear. "Then watch your movie on one of them!"

"Is this why you called?" I asked.

"Nah, baby. Wanted to make sure you were ready. I'll send the car to your place now."

"Oh." I looked down at my outfit, then I cringed.

Your first thought is how you look? Seriously, Val?

"I'll be ready in five minutes."

"Clive will be there in ten."

He hung up but not before I heard renewed shouting on his end. I shook my head as I headed upstairs to change. I may have understood why they were friends, but that didn't make them any less of an odd bunch.

I didn't have much time so I hurried into a pair of jeans and a silk blouse Mom bought me for my birthday. What I wore did not matter, but it had been a while since I had been in Ryder's house and no time at all since I had hooked up with Jaxson. Worrying about clothes and jewelry saved me a few minutes of having to think about *that*.

Clive was waiting outside when I walked out. The drive to Ryder's house was short, but my fretting made it longer. Were we finally going to talk about Scarlett? The Spades? What happens now? What happened back then? Would I ever shake the feeling that there was more to Walter McMillian's death? Did everyone who tangled with the Spades end tragically? And if that was true, what would happen to me?

My head was a mess when Clive finally spat me out in Ryder's drive. I tried to sort through it all as I climbed the steps. The door opened before I raised my hand to knock.

"Hello, Miss Moon. We are expecting you."

I blinked at the tall, bald stranger. "Do I know you?"

"You do not. My name is Mr. Grange. I am the Sheas' butler. If you would follow me, the master and his guests are on the terrace."

He took off at the end of his sentence and I hurried to stay on his heels.

The Shea mansion was more magnificent than I remembered. Twice the size of Sofia's place, the place screamed wealth so loud it deafened anyone who walked inside. It didn't escape my thoughts that this could all be Adam's, but it went as quickly as it came. That happy baby did not need any of this. Ryder grew up here and happy was far from what he was.

Grange led me through the multitude of rooms until we reached the sliding glass door. He bowed slightly as he held it open for me.

"Thank you," I said absentmindedly. I was already fixed on the sight of Maverick, Ezra, and Jaxson surrounding someone I hadn't expected to see: Caroline.

The older woman reclined in a lounge chair by the pool, although she was in full dress. The long-sleeved linen dress looked lovely on her, but it covered every inch of her pale skin except for her face and hands. Shielding her from the nice day were a pair of thick sunglasses, floppy hat, a large parasol, and the man that had been an ever-present shadow for as long as I could remember. I didn't know if Jacob was a bodyguard or what, but whenever Caroline emerged from her bedroom, he was nearby.

I drifted closer to the group.

"...be excited now that summer is here," said Caroline. "Tell me everything you've done."

"Ricky went to football camp," Jaxson replied. "Ezra and I went on vacation with our parents."

She hummed. "Did you go anywhere exciting?"

"Mom."

I jumped. I hadn't even heard the doors open behind me. Ryder passed me by holding a tray weighted down with a single glass.

"Guys, stop crowding her. Go away."

"They aren't crowding me, my love," Caroline protested as the boys stood up. "I love talking with your friends."

"Why? They suck."

"You suck, Eugene!" Jaxson shouted back.

"My middle name is not Eugene!"

Caroline placed a thin hand on Ryder's arm. "Don't shout, son."

"Sorry, Mom."

Jaxson delivered the final blow by throwing his middle fingers up all the way to the door. I clapped my hand over my mouth to cover my laugh. I could have gone inside with them, but something pulled me closer to mother and son.

Caroline beamed at him. "Is that for me?"

"Yes." He set the lemonade on the small table beside her. "Can I get you anything else?"

He's so attentive to her.

It shouldn't have surprised me. Ryder was always good to his mom even while he was his most beastly to me. Despite that, seeing his kind side still shook me.

"You can sit with me."

"In a minute. I'm making you soup and a sandwich for lunch. It's almost ready."

Her smile was fond as she gazed at him. "We have a chef for that."

"He doesn't make it the way you like it. I heard you say so."

"So, of course, my love steps in to make it right. Where would I be without you?"

"You won't find out." Ryder bent and kissed her cheek. He turned and froze as if noticing me for the first time. "Valentina."

"Valentina?" Caroline gifted me with her smile. "Hello, dear. You'll sit with me, won't you?"

"Mo—"

"Yes, I will." I crossed over to her without hesitation, claiming the seat Ezra vacated. "How are you?"

"Very well." She said that, but Caroline Shea looked as thin and frail as she always did. I got the feeling that so much as a tight hug would shatter her into pieces. She glanced at Ryder. "Go on, love. Don't let the food burn."

I could read the reluctance on his face, but he didn't argue with her. When he was gone, she turned to Jacob. "Would you give us some privacy, please?" The silent man backed away without protest.

"It's good to see you, Valentina. I hope you've been well too."

"I have. It was my birthday yesterday. We went to this fancy restaurant." The words poured from my lips unbidden. I couldn't help it. Something about Caroline's open face made you want to speak to her. "We had a great time."

"That's wonderful. I was worried there was something wrong when you asked to be put in touch with a hacker and assigned a bodyguard from my personal staff."

"A few issues with people at school, but they're settled now."
More or less.

"That's good news." She leaned back, getting comfortable. "So tell me about young Adam."

"He's two now. He likes books about magical forests and screaming my name at the top of his lungs."

She laughed. It was a soft sound that managed to shake her whole body. "My Ryder was the same. He'd scream for me even when he could see me. He wanted me close by at all times. Boys and their mothers."

"I can't picture baby Ryder," I said with a laugh. "My brain can't conjure up chubby cheeks and a round bottom."

Caroline covered her mouth to hide her mirth. "My son had the chubbiest cheeks. He was truly quite fat and I've got the pictures to prove it."

"I'd like to see those."

Giggling, she swatted my knee like we were indulging in something sneaky. What Caroline Shannon Shea and I had couldn't be described as friendship. We barely spoke outside of hidden texts, and I knew very little about her life. She was kind in every way, and yet, I had no clue why she married that brute Benjamin Shea, or the demons she fought every day. She wasn't my friend, but it was like Jaxson said. Sometimes big things happen that bind the most unlikely people together.

Ryder returned with a tray of food and it brought our conversation to a halt. Caroline grabbed his hand when he set it down.

"Ryder, go and get your baby pictures."

He went rigid, half doubled over. "What?"

"Valentina wants to see you when you were little." She looked at me. "I have the most adorable one when he was a month old. You can see his little round bottom."

I snorted a laugh as Ryder seized my hand.

"There's no time for that, Mom." Ryder pulled me to my feet. "Everyone is waiting for us."

"But—"

"Eat, Mom," Ryder said, cutting through my protest. "I'll come back and sit with you after."

"Alright." She waved us off as her shadow returned to her side again.

"What were you two talking about?" Ryder asked the minute we stepped inside. "Why do you want to see my pictures?"

"I don't— I mean, I wouldn't mind seeing them. It was just an offhand comment." I turned away, scanning for the rest of the guys. "Where is everyone?"

"In my room."

"Then let's go." I made to leave, but a hand stopped me. "Ryder, what—" I paused when I saw the look on his face.

"My mom..." He looked to be forcing each word out. "...did she ever tell you who..."

"Your father was?"

He nodded.

"No," I replied softly. "She never said and I never asked. Do you want me to ask her?"

His hair fell across his eyes as he shook his head.

"Will you talk to her?"

"I can't without revealing how I know. It's up to her to tell me."

"I'm sorry." It didn't feel like enough, but what else could I say?

He released me. "We should go."

It was me who led the way to his room. It was funny how well I remembered the clown painting where I took a right. The slight scratch on the door for the bathroom. Then at the end of the hall, Ryder's room.

The boys were waiting inside. Jaxson laid out on Ryder's bed like he owned it. Maverick sat at his computer, and Ezra checked out his bookshelves. Except for them, everything was perfect, spotless, bordering on sterile. There were photos, of course, and awards and medals, but I never felt like any of this said a thing about the real Ryder, not like his room at the academy did.

Jaxson propped himself up on his elbows and patted the spot next to him. Smiling, I went to sit at his side. He rested his head in my lap and got comfortable.

I looked up and saw Ezra watching us. He looked away when I caught his glance. "We're all here. Let's talk."

"About Scarlett." I didn't say it as a question. "What's going to happen now?"

"Nothing happened after she— after she disappeared," said Jaxson. "Everyone accepted that she resigned and took off."

"But there are still too many questions." Maverick swung the desk chair around to face us. "Who is she? How did she become a Spade? And are there others?"

"I think we can be sure that she picked us to be Knights," Ezra spoke up. "To keep us nice and under her thumb. The four boys who knew her secret."

"What if she is the only one?" Maverick added. "What if there always was a single Spade who ran the school until they chose someone else to take their place?"

Ryder finally spoke up. "This is all just guessing. We don't know any more about the Spades than we did before, and the only one who could have told us is dead."

Jaxson lifted his head. "We know that Scarlett marked Valentina and we know why. If she had more Spade buddies, do you wanna bet that she didn't tell them the reason? 'Hey, the new girl may know that I'm a pedophile, let's get rid of her.'"

Maverick inclined his head. "That's true. If there were others she needed to explain it to, then she would have made something up."

"Then this would be over if they knew the truth."

All eyes flew to me.

"That's where this is going, right?" I continued. "If she was the only Spade, then this is over, but we can't be sure of that. If there are others, they would need to know the truth of why she marked me to back off. Maybe they would take back the mark themselves, if that's a thing."

"I've never heard of a mark being taken back," Ezra said slowly. "But you're also the first person to last this long. The others left right away and McMillian—"

"—was killed," I finished. "Killed because the Spades thought that was the only way to end it, but if they knew I was never a threat in the first place, this could end another way."

"But they can't know," Ezra protested. "No one knows what she did to— Not even my mom." He tossed his head. "I'm not telling—"

"You don't have to." I slid out from under Jaxson and stood. "I'll say it was me. Scarlett went too far with me and when I threatened to tell Evergreen, I wound up marked. People will believe it. They know I hung out in her class alone, and they probably overheard all the times she called me pretty or touched me."

Maverick got to his feet. "Val, you don't have to—"

"Do you have a better idea?" I stepped into the middle of the room and met each of their eyes. "I can't go the next two years always looking over my shoulder with bodyguards on my tail. If I can end this now, then I have to do it. Even if this doesn't stop the Spades, then it might stop the rest of the students. They wouldn't keep attacking me if they knew they were doing it under the orders of a predator."

Ryder stepped in front of me, filling my vision as he blocked everyone else out. "That would turn the school against the Spades... and you know what happened to the last guy who did that."

I swallowed hard. "I'll take that risk."

"What if we won't?" I felt Jaxson's hand on my waist. I let him turn me to face him. "What if I can't stand for you to be a target anymore?"

I pressed my hand to his cheek, heart aching for what we all knew I had to say.

"We don't have a choice."

Chapter Three

"I can drive you down so your mom doesn't have to make the trip." Sofia rested on my bed, feet in the air, as I packed. "It'll be fun. We'll blast the music the whole ride."

"That would be fun." I tossed in my last dress and plopped down next to her. "But Mom and I were planning to make a day of it. A new waterpark opened up between here and home so we're taking Adam. We're packing in as much stuff before I'm locked away in Evergreen."

"Okay, I get it. Although, I think this year will be a lot more fun."

"Why? Because you're hot and heavy with Zane?"

Looking at her upside down, I still didn't miss her smirk. "That is one reason, but I meant that the juniors and seniors get more freedom. Later curfew. More weekend passes. Plus the school trips. Last year, the junior class *would* have gone to Aspen for winter break if the headmaster hadn't had a meltdown. This year, I hope he keeps it together long enough for us to go."

"That would be amazing. I've never been that far before."

"We'll totally share a room. Go skiing together. Sip hot chocolate in front of the fire. It'll be epic."

My smile was tinged with sadness. "That would be epic, Sof, but until I'm sure the mark is off my back, it can't happen."

"Oh, yeah. I've been waiting till the last minute to tell you this so here goes. I'm not pretending we're not friends anymore. No matter what happens, I'm on your side. Don't argue with me."

I sprang up, narrowly missing knocking our heads together. "But, Sofia! This is dangerous! Someone tried to burn me alive, throw me down the stairs, and drop a planter on my head. Until I know—"

"Didn't I say not to argue with me?" She grabbed me and shoved. I went back down with a yelp as she put her head on my chest. "This is why I waited because you'd try to talk me out of it. I'm not stupid. I know it's dangerous, but I'm done, Val."

"You're sweet as honey," I replied, remembering something Jaxson said. "I'm ruthless. If they come after you, it'll be too much."

"Sweet as honey?" She laughed. "I'm tougher than you think. Plus, you're not changing my mind. If you're so worried about me, then we work harder to get rid of the mark."

"Trust me, I'm trying."

Ring. Ring.

"That'll be Olivia." I wrapped my arms around her and squeezed. "Thank you for letting me stay. I had so much fun."

"Me too."

We hopped up to get my things. One stop to say goodbye to her parents and then we headed out to meet Mom.

"Everything will be different this year," she said as she hugged me once more. "I promise."

"EXCITED FOR SCHOOL, kid?"

"That's one word for it." The line of cars crested over the hill. It was move-in day. The students of Evergreen had returned. "This year is going to be intense. We have to start prepping for college. Grades are everything this year."

"You already know where you want to go. Somerset University so you can be close to Adam."

I twisted around to see him. The baby was engrossed with his toy train. "It's an hour away from home, but it's also one of the top-rated schools in the country. It'll be difficult to get in even with Evergreen Academy on my application. Can you tell I'm freaking?"

"I can and you don't have to. You're getting in. I know it."

I was glad one of us was confident. The truth was I had no idea what this year would bring. That day at Ryder's house with the Knights hadn't answered any questions. We argued my plan in circles before Caroline called up asking for her son and we all went home.

This had to end... and I'll be the one to do it.

Soon we arrived at the gates and the staff sprang into action. They took my belongings while I said my goodbyes to Mom and Adam.

As her horn faded, it was replaced by the clacks of leather shoes, rolling of suitcases, and the shouts of people who hadn't seen each other for weeks meeting up. The gates of Evergreen stood open and proud, glinting in the gilded sun and ready to welcome me to another year of unknowns.

I sighed. "Let's do this."

Students raced past in all directions as I headed for my lone building. I was actually looking forward to being back in my quiet space. I didn't like a lot of things about Evergreen, but the dorms weren't one of them.

The noise fell away as I crossed the courtyard and stepped onto the dew-soaked grass. I saw him immediately, but I didn't pick up my pace. When we were a foot apart, he spoke.

"Hey, Moon."

"Ezra."

The taller boy leaned against my doorframe; his expression blank.

"I know why you're here," I began.

He raised a brow. "You do?"

"Yes." I moved in closer until his heady scent overwhelmed me. "You came clean to my mom because you want me to do the same. Tell her that you didn't lay a finger on me."

"I came clean because it was the right thing to do." Ezra's face became tight. "You came through for us. Because of you, I never have to walk through the same halls as that woman again. Sit in her class while she smiles and pats my head until it's everything I can do not to throw up. Scarlett used us to hurt you and... I'll never forgive myself for playing her game.

"I deserved a lot worse than an afternoon doing yardwork after what I did. I hate what Mom thinks of me now, but honestly, I don't think much more of myself, so tell her or don't. I'm a piece of shit anyway."

Ezra was right. I wasn't expecting that at all. I gazed at him, trying to find the right words to respond. I opened my mouth.

"Want to come in?"

Ezra blinked. I blinked.

I don't think either of us knew I was going to say that, but now that it was out there.

"Come in," I repeated. "I want to talk inside."

I opened the door and walked in, expecting Ezra to follow. From the footsteps I heard behind me, he was. The two of us heeded the noise coming from upstairs and walked in on the staff putting my things in my room.

"Thank you. I've got it from here."

They inclined their heads and filed out, leaving us alone. For a while, Ezra and I just looked at each other across the plush gray rug.

"I'll tell her," I said, finally breaking the silence. "I'll admit to Amelia that you didn't hit me. We were both hurt by Scarlett. Because of her, you struck at me, but I struck back. I got my revenge and I'm satisfied, there's no reason it needs to go on now that we both know the truth. Besides, you're an asshole, but you don't go around beating women and your mother shouldn't think you do."

Ezra dropped his gaze. "Thank you."

I went over to my bed and sat down. "So what now?"

"I've... still got two more 'labors' to do." Ezra took a step and then stopped. He looked around like he was wondering where to be.

"You can sit down on the bed." After a slight hesitation, he did so. "So what do you have in mind for the next two? I know Mom appreciated someone finally getting at those gutters."

He cracked a smile. "Not sure yet. Jaxson said he took you to Interstellar and that's hard to beat. News sets aren't that interesting."

"We don't have to do anything like that. I just appreciated that he thought of something he knew I would love."

He nodded. Ezra wasn't looking at me; he seemed fixed on a spot on my rug.

"Are you two together?"

I started. "What? Who?"

"You and Jaxson." He still wasn't looking at me. "Are you with him now?"

My jaw worked as I tried to form an answer. It was a good question. I had been all set to have sex with Jaxson Van Zandt. Things had changed between us; I couldn't deny that.

"No," I said in the end. "We haven't talked or made anything official, so no, we're not together."

"Do you want to be with him?"

"I want to get through this year and get into Somerset University. Everything else I'll figure out as I go along."

"Alright."

I thought he might say more, but nothing came. The silence spread between us like spilled tea until I couldn't take it anymore.

"Can I be honest?" I asked.

"Sure."

"What I would like is to get to know you."

That made him pick up his head. "What?"

"I get Jaxson, Maverick, even Ryder, but I've never understood you. You keep your real self so hidden. I want to get to know that person."

"How do you know this isn't my real self?"

"Is it?" I challenged.

He didn't reply.

"That's what I thought." I scooted closer to him. "You want to make it up to me—want my trust. Then you have to trust me too. No more mannequin man; I want Ezra Lennox."

"You might not like him." Those words were said so softly they nearly didn't reach my ears.

"I'll risk it."

Ezra tilted his head back, studying me. "That is really all you want?"

"Yes." I held my breath.

"Okay." Ezra heaved himself off the bed. "I have to go. See you around, Moon."

I didn't stop him. The door closed behind Ezra leaving me more mixed up than ever. I couldn't help but remember what Jaxson said. There never was a bet between the Knights to bed the new girl. The kiss I shared with Ezra at the masquerade ball was real, but it ended because of the same thing we were trying to overcome now. I wanted to know the real him.

But how will things change between us when I do?

I LET MY TOWEL FALL to the floor as I held up my uniform choices. Red was the color for our junior year. I had been wearing the skirt and blazer as a mark of rebellion—purposely standing out so they would all know I wouldn't accept their shit.

The war is over now. At least it is for me. I'll have to make everyone accept it.

Mind made up, I tossed the skirt on the bed and donned the dress. It looked so much better than the hideous yellow mess of last year that I had fun picking out earrings and bracelets to go with it. When I stepped out of my dorm, I knew I looked fierce.

A new year meant a new floor, and my feet carried me through the halls of the main building to the elevator that would take me to junior hall. I swiped my card on the reader and the elevator rumbled to life.

I stepped out into the well-known chaos of the first day. Everyone walked past hunting down lockers and room numbers that most didn't notice me. I took the anonymity for the win it was and went in search of my locker.

370. 374. 37—

I scanned the rows until I landed on my best friend. Sofia leaned against the locker, grinning up at a guy whose tie she was twirling around her finger. I had met Zane Thomas a few times. Sofia had snuck him in over the summer whenever her parents were out. I didn't wonder what she saw in the guy.

He was tall and well-built from years of rugby, and sported the cutest mop of curly brown hair. Then, of course, there were the eyes. I had never met anyone with hazel eyes before him, and I was glad of it. Those things were lethal. Sofia turned to goo whenever they sparkled at her. Throw in the accent and she broke her six-month no-sex streak a week after meeting him.

I stepped up to them, and sure enough, my locker was the one they were standing by. Sofia took her eyes off Zane. "Hey, Val. What's up?"

I pointed. "This is my locker. Are we neighbors?"

"No, we are." Zane's smile shone on me. "This is great. I heard we have the same classes too." Zane flicked Sofia's nose. "This one is way smarter than me so she's got higher math and science classes."

"She's smarter than all of us, Zane. None of us stand a chance."

Sofia giggled. "Stop it, guys. We have most of the same classes, and we're sitting together at lunch whether Val likes it or not."

We faced off, staring each other down. Sofia wouldn't move on telling everyone we were friends. Zane looked between the both of us.

"Um, why wouldn't she like it?"

We dropped the stare-off and replaced them with hesitant looks. Neither of us had told him about being marked, the Spades, none of it. It all sounded so insane. How do we begin to explain it?

Sofia took a breath. "Look, Zane. This school is—"

"Zane!"

Three pairs of eyes looked down the hallway and landed on a vaguely familiar-looking guy. His red blazer was slung over his shoulder as he loped down the hall, scattering students like bowling pins. They skirted out of his way as he marched up to Zane.

"Where the fuck is Markham's class? I've walked up and down these halls five times."

I blinked at him. He definitely wasn't familiar to me, but that accent was.

"Ladies." Zane clapped the guy on his shoulder. "This is my twin, Kai. Fraternal twin, obviously. He's shorter, uglier, and a lot less charming."

To my surprise, Kai burst out laughing. "What do you mean shorter and uglier? Girls don't go for that bug-eyed, praying mantis thing you have going on."

I smothered a laugh as Sofia stuck her head out from behind Zane. "I do."

Kai didn't lose his grin. "That's only because you met him first."

The laugh ripped from my lips before I could stop it and Kai glanced at me. "She'll back me up." Suddenly, his arm was around my shoulder and he was pulling me in. "Which one of the Thomas twins would you choose?"

A flush crept up my cheeks. They were both gorgeous no matter what either of them said. They both had curly hair and hazel eyes, but that's where the similarities stopped. Kai was shorter than his twin, but inches above me. His face was sharper, his lips fuller, and all of it added up to one seriously attractive dude.

Not that I was going to say that to a person I knew for less than three minutes. I also wasn't going to say I'd go for my best friend's boyfriend.

"There is no way answering that would be good for me."

"Stop making Valentina uncomfortable, idiot." Zane put his hand on his brother's face and shoved. He stumbled back, taking me with him. "Let's go, Sofia."

Sofia tossed me a wave and took off with Zane, leaving me alone with Kai.

"Sorry about that guy."

Chuckling, I shrugged off his arm. "Right. Because Zane was the problem."

"Zane's been the problem since he hogged all the space in my mother's womb." He held up his schedule. "So how about it? Will you show me how to get to Markham's class?"

"Sure. I'm going that way anyway." I set off and Kai fell in beside me. "We had her for freshman year. I'm surprised she moved up. It's hard for anyone to do that in this school."

"What's she like?"

"Tough, but if you fly under the radar she doesn't give you grief." I cut eyes to him. "What are *you* like?"

"Me?"

I nodded. "You and your brother are the first new additions to our class since me. What's your story?"

Those hazel orbs swept over my face. "Want to know my story? Here it is: Once upon a time, there was a boy living in Cape Town with his parents, twin, and beautiful girlfriend. The boy's father got a new job in the States and ripped said boy away from his friends and the girl he loved to live in a pretentious hellhole in the middle of nowhere. The end."

This would have been the part where I said Evergreen wasn't so bad, and he would love it here, but me of all people couldn't say that. "I'm sorry. That sucks."

"It does." He looked away. "But I'm here now, in this school, walking with you, so tell me about yourself."

I considered for a second. *You know what, why not tell the truth?*

"This is my third year here, and in my first, I was marked because I saw something I shouldn't. Ever since, I've been harassed, taunted, bullied, and almost killed three times. Four seventeen-year-old boys rule this school. They are the Knights and everyone is afraid to go against them. Behind the scenes are the Spades, and they strike even more fear. This school is way more than a pretentious hellhole. It's like nowhere you've ever been before, or will ever be."

Kai gaped at me. "Is this one of your American jokes? Because I've never understood your humor."

I smiled despite myself. "No, it's all true. If you don't believe me, ask anyone. They'll tell you the same." I glanced past him. "This is Markham's class."

He turned to look. "Thank you, Valentina." When he glanced back, he was grinning. "You're a strange one. We'll get along well."

Shaking my head, I followed him inside. Markham's desk sat empty while around us students found their seats and their friends. Kai made to turn down the row. "Kai, wait. You have to put your phone in here." The no-phone ban may have been repealed, but we still weren't allowed them during the day. Kai stepped up to the phone box with me. "Put it in the slot with your student id."

"Why can't we have our phones?"

"It's the rules."

"That's stupid."

"Trust me, it used to be a lot worse. Take the win, Kai."

He laughed. "Whatever you say, but now I'm choosing you as my student guide."

"Don't you already have one of those?"

Kai scoffed. "Some girl named Isabella who showed up, handed me my schedule, and told me to figure it out." He peered over his shoulder. "She's over there."

I followed his line of sight. Isabella leaned against the window flocked by her usual crowd, the Diamonds.

Yep. This whole one big class thing was a huge mistake.

"I know Isabella," I said simply. I tapped his arm. "Come on, let's grab seats."

Sofia waved us over to their spot near the back. She and Zane sat next to each other with two empty desks in front of them. I plopped down in front of Sofia while Kai sat by Zane.

She leaned in. "Isabella was running her mouth before you got here. Someone asked if she lost her spot as head of the Diamonds since you beat her, and that set off a rant about hip-hop and ballet not being in the same league, and your win not counting. She'll have to be shoved off the throne, because she's not stepping down."

"She can stay." I made sure my voice didn't carry. "I never wanted to lead that pack of jackals, I only wanted her to spend her days as queen knowing that deep down she was a loser—beaten by the girl from the Wakefield slum she thought she was so much better than."

She whistled. "Damn, girl. You are ruthless."

"Fear me, Sofia. Fear me."

We fell out giggling and the boys gave us looks.

"Can we know the joke?" Kai asked.

"You're going to be the joke if you don't hop out of that seat, playboy."

My laughter dried up quick. I gaped at Jaxson as Kai's eyes narrowed into slits. "Who the fuck are you?"

Jaxson's face matched his so exactly you would have thought they were the twins. "Who the fuck are *you*?"

"Jaxson, they're new students," Sofia said quickly. "They just moved here."

"That's no excuse for not knowing the rules. I'll be sitting next to Val, so get up."

Kai looked at me as my cheeks heated up. *Everyone* was looking at me now.

"I'm not going anywhere," Kai said, although his gaze was on me. There was something in his expression that I couldn't read. "So fuck off."

"Kai!" Sofia hissed.

This was quickly getting out of hand. I grabbed Jaxson's arm. "It's fine, Jaxson. Just find another seat."

Jaxson twisted and caught my hand. Before I could react, he pressed his lips to my fingers. "You going to stand for this, baby? You don't want to sit with me?"

My eyes traveled down to his exposed chest, and a vision of us half-naked on the couch flashed through my mind. I wanted to do more than sit with him, but Kai was cool; I couldn't let him unwittingly put a target on his back.

"I do, but I'm his student guide. I have to stick close."

He seemed to accept this. "Then find me when you shake him loose." He kissed my hand again before claiming a seat further up. I placed my hand in my lap, rubbing my fingers over the spot where he kissed me. It tingled in the most distracting way.

"That your boyfriend?"

I jumped. "What?"

Kai jerked his head in Jaxson's direction. "You two going out?"

"No." I shook out my hand. "He's not my boyfriend."

"Does *he* know that?"

I opened my mouth and nothing came out. Did he know that? *Time for a subject change.*

"Kai, he is who I was telling you about. One of the four boys who rule the school."

"Rule the school?" Zane made a face at Sofia. "What's going on?"

She sighed. "Okay, so over a hundred years ago..."

"ADVANCED GOVERNMENT, Advanced Literature and Composition, precalculus, Spanish, speech, orchestra, gym, and Advanced Chemistry. Is your schedule as horrible?"

I handed Kai mine. "I don't have speech, but yes, we're in the same boat."

"I didn't want to be in advanced. There wasn't an option for anything else."

Kai, Zane, and I strode through the halls for precalc. Sofia went off to Calculus II while the boys stuck by my side. Which was a surprise. I was sure they'd be the ones to shake me loose when they heard the whole story.

"It won't be so bad. We can study together... if you're not afraid of hanging with someone who's marked."

Kai snorted. "That bullshit? I'm not letting some playing card tell me who my friends are, and I can't believe anyone else here did either."

"For once I agree with him," echoed Zane. "Bullshit is exactly what that is."

"You won't catch me disagreeing with you. The problem is everyone else does."

"Fuck them." Kai said that with such certainty it pulled me up short. "I'm not dropping you, and you know what, if anyone pulls anything, I'll kick their ass. I don't like bullies."

"And again, I agree with my brother. No one is messing with you this year, Valentina. That's a promise."

"I can take care of myself, guys, but... thank you. I really appreciate it."

We were walking for a while before I realized we had picked up a fourth party. Ezra strolled alongside us like it was no big deal.

"Lennox? What are you doing?"

"What are you doing?" he shot back. "Tonight."

Ezra headed off to the side and I went with him, waving the boys on. "What's going on tonight?" I looked him up and down, noting how perfectly put together he was. His red blazer was buttoned. His leather shoes polished, and his hair slicked back.

I had the sudden urge to run my fingers through his hair—see what it looked like wild and messy.

"That's up to you," he said. "If you want... we can do number two tonight."

I knew what that meant. Ezra was ready to let me peek inside. How could I say no to that?

"I want."

"Okay. I'll pick you up at your door at nine." Ezra took a step. "Wait. You're not skipping out on lunch today, right?"

"No. Why?"

"You just need to be there."

He walked off before I could get another question out. Shaking my head, I joined the twins who stood off to the side to wait for me.

Whatever it is, I'll find out.

I TOSSED MY GYM CLOTHES in the locker under Coach Panzer's watchful eye. Another rule that stuck around for junior year was that we weren't allowed to be in the locker room if she wasn't there. The headmaster didn't want us planning any more drug deals or arranging to buy term papers.

"Hurry up, ladies. We all want our lunch."

"Val doesn't." A loathsome hiss slipped into my ear, alerting me to her presence. "She'll only throw it up after."

"Still on that." I didn't pause in getting dressed. "Didn't we leave the thin jokes in freshman year? Get new material, Natalie."

"Get fucked, Moon. Oh wait, no one is trying to get with a diseased slut."

A chorus of laughter broke out behind me.

"Ladies!" Panzer's shout broke through the cackling. "Get dressed, and get going."

I listened to the slamming and shuffling of people walking away. A presence pressed in on me.

"You better watch your back," Natalie whispered. Her finger brushed the ridges of my spine, making me shiver in disgust. "You're going to pay for what you did to me last year."

"I told you, dumbass. I didn't plant that phone."

"I know it was you!"

"I never left my seat." I slammed the locker shut and spun to face her. Natalie's face was bright red with the strain of holding herself back. "So why don't you spend your time figuring out *who else* wanted to take you down. I'm sure there are plenty of people."

"You're such a—"

A shadow fell over us. I snapped my head up and got the full force of Panzer's scowl.

"Did you two not hear me? Get dressed!"

"Yes, Coach."

I scrambled to put on the rest of my clothes and got out. I passed by my locker on the way to the cafeteria and found Sofia, Zane, and Kai milling about.

"What's up, guys?"

Sofia poked her head out from under Zane's arm. "We were waiting for you."

"Why?"

"'Cause we're walking in together. We're getting our food together. Then we're sitting together."

I opened my mouth.

"Get on board, Moon," Kai said, "or Sofia says I get to steal your dessert."

I laughed. "I was only going to say I love you guys. Come on, and if any of you touches my dessert, you're losing a hand."

Striding side by side with them through the hostile stares, I felt so many emotions it was hard to keep track of it all. Anxiety was strong among them. I didn't want anyone to be hurt because of me, but more than that, I was grateful. I was fit to burst at having friends like this that would stand by me when everyone else abandoned me.

We walked through the doors like nothing was up, chatting away. "The food here is way too healthy," Sofia said. "Good, but there's nothing deep-fried in sight. We used to have soda, but Evergreen took it away."

"It's still pretty good even though my best friend never lets me have dessert," I added.

Sofia made a face at me. "You lose your dessert fair and—"

"Sofia? What are you doing?"

I stiffened at the voice.

Our group shifted to face the others that approached us. Eric led the pack with Paisley and Claire on either side. All three of them looked at Sofia like they had never seen her before.

Claire's eyes flicked to me. "Sofia, we're sitting by the window. Let's go."

"No." Sofia folded her arms, staring them down. "I'm sitting with Val. She's my best friend and always has been. I'm tired of pretending to go along with this marked stuff."

Eric's eyes bugged out. "W-what are you talking about?! You mean you've been lying to us the whole time?"

"I— Yes, and I'm sorry. You're my friends too and I love you guys, but all of this is wrong, and I can't do it anymore. If you get that, then you'll sit with us. If not..."

She trailed off, letting her words hang in the air. It was the tensest minute of my life waiting to see what the people I used to call my friends would do. Paisley, so pretty and fierce, looked at me and something flickered in her eyes. She took a step.

"No." Eric's hand flashed out and secured Paisley's wrist. "It sucks what happened to Valentina, but we can't afford to be next.

We won't risk our families or businesses by getting the Spades to turn on us. These are the traditions of the school, and if she didn't like it, she could have left."

My eyes narrowed. "Want to stop talking about me like I'm not standing right here, Eric?"

To my surprise, Eric turned and faced me head-on. "I'm sorry, Val, but we're not friends anymore, and we haven't been for two years. You're marked. That's not going to change."

I looked at the other girls. "You feel the same way?"

Paisley actually looked like she would cry. "I can't be marked too, Val. I'm sorry."

"And you, Claire?"

Claire's gaze was clear and steady. "We're from the same place, so you know more than anyone here how hard it is to get out. I've got a family too, and they're depending on me. Bye, Val."

Claire was the first to walk away. Eric and Paisley went after her. I glanced at Sofia in time to see her wipe away a stray tear. This hit her harder than it did me. I accepted a long time ago that those three were no longer my friends, but I know she wanted to believe they were better than this.

We were a quiet group as we got our lunch trays and found a table near the dais, as far away from the window as possible. Kai was the first to speak.

"They're really serious about this marked stuff here."

I could feel all the eyes on us. "Very serious. This is your chance to walk away."

Kai leaned over and plucked my cheesecake off the tray.

"Hey!"

He took a massive bite, grinning at me as he chewed. "You were warned, Moon. Stop telling us to walk away. I'm not going anywhere."

Hiding my smile, I started eating the lunch I had left. It took a minute, but eventually, we fell into normal conversation, ignoring the rest of the juniors. I was making short work of my cauliflower rice burrito when the Knights strolled inside. The hush that accompanied their presence fell over the room. They stepped up to the dais trailed by the girls who delivered their lunch. The girls set down the trays, but the guys didn't sit.

There was a shift in the air as the Knights spread out across the dais, looking out across the room.

What's going on?

"Listen up," Jaxson called. "We have something to say."

Silence fell before he finished the sentence. All eyes were on them, mine included.

Maverick stepped forward. "Two years ago, Valentina Moon was marked."

My chair screeched across the tile as I rose from my seat. *What is this? What are they doing?*

"Everyone did what they were supposed to do," Ezra continued. "Tried to drive her out."

Jaxson spoke up. "Now there are new orders from us and we'll make sure the freshmen, sophomores, and seniors know too."

"It's over," Ryder stated. "The mark is lifted. Valentina Moon can stay."

My jaw dropped as all around me, chaos erupted.

Chapter Four

"Can you believe this? Did you know they were going to do this?"

"No."

"Val, this is so great." Sofia seized me in a hug that about cracked my ribs. "It's finally over. Finally."

I put my arms around her and hugged back. It had been a bizarre day to be sure. Of course, the Knights' announcement was good news, but I had no clue it was coming. I had a plan. I was going to start small, spreading the rumor of Scarlett trying to force herself on me and the mark following soon after. I wanted the students to connect the dots and let it grow like wildfire until everyone knew what she truly was. At least, that was what I told the Knights I would do, despite their objections.

I had classes with them, but the school day ended with me not able to corner any of them. We needed to talk.

"What are you doing tonight?" Sofia asked. "We should celebrate. We can go up to the roof."

"I'm supposed to meet Ezra tonight, but we can hang out until then. Just let me drop my stuff in my room."

"Okay. Come to the junior dorm. I've stashed a family-size bag of chips and a pack of soda. We'll have a mini-movie marathon."

"Deal."

I left her and headed off for Markham's class. She was sitting at her desk when I arrived. No one else was inside.

The tip-tapping on her keyboard ceased. "Miss Moon, how are you?"

"I'm good." I rescued my phone from the box.

"I heard of the announcement made in the lunchroom."

"I guess everyone has by now."

"You must be very happy."

I didn't reply. The truth was I didn't know what to think.

"This is the first time in school history that something like this has happened," she continued. "Did you know they were going to do this?"

"I was as surprised as anyone."

"Why do you think they decided to do it?"

I lifted my head, studying her. "Does it matter? All I care about is that this is over. You must be happy too. You don't have to look the other way anymore."

Wrinkles formed around her mouth as her lips tightened. "I never wanted to look the other way. I did as much as I could to help you."

I did not want to get into what I thought of that. "I have to get going. Someone is waiting for me."

"Of course, Miss Moon."

I walked out, saying no more. The afternoon sun lit the cobblestone courtyard and cast its shades of reds and golds on me as I walked to my dorm. I loved it out here, even though the space was tinged with the memory of Jaxson knocking me out of the way of the falling planter that would have ended my life.

I passed through onto the grass and my eyes lit on him. It was as though thoughts of him had conjured him up. I couldn't help the smile that spread across my lips as Jaxson came to meet me, enfolding me in his arms.

"Hey, baby."

I sunk into his chest, breathing deeply his sweet spicy scent. I can't believe I ever hated being called baby.

"Jaxson." His haze was trying to pull me under, but I had to stay clear. "We need to talk."

"We do? About what?"

I pulled back until his arms fell at his side. "Today in the cafeteria, why did you guys do that? We had a plan. The school was supposed to find out the truth about Scarlett and turn on the Spades themselves."

His gaze sharpened. "Or the Spades figured out your plan and turned on *you* themselves. None of us were willing to risk that. This way, if there are more Spades, they'll look at us, not you. We're Knights, we're protected. Especially now that Scarlett is gone. There isn't much they can do to us."

"You don't know that," I protested. "There is plenty an unseen enemy can do. The Spades could be literally anyone. They could be *teaching* us and we wouldn't know."

"It's done now, mama." Jaxson's face softened as he brushed my hair behind my ear. "We have spoken to all the grades. They mess with you; they deal with us."

I wanted to argue some more, but deep down I knew he was right. It was too late now.

"I can still spread the truth about Scarlett. The world should know what she truly was."

"If people start looking too hard at her; they might question her disappearance. We don't want that."

I clenched my fists. He was right. I *hated* that he was right. "So... it's over."

"Yes, baby. It's over."

His hand traveled down my neck. I didn't stop him as he drew me in.

I melted into the kiss, letting the fear and tension leak out of my body. He broke it and rested his head on mine while I worked to form words again.

"Does he know he's not your boyfriend?"

The words were a dagger to my balloon of happiness. My eyes snapped open. "Jaxson, we have to talk."

"Again?"

"Yes." Taking a deep breath, I stepped out of his hold. "It's about us."

"What about us?" He looked so adorably confused, I wanted to kiss away the wrinkle in his brow. Then keep kissing all the way down until I got to his—

Stop it, Moon! Focus!

"Jaxson, things got really intense between us over the summer and I don't regret any of it. If I could have done things over again, I would do it the same except I would have flung your phone across the room."

He chuckled. "I wish every day I had."

"But—"

"Why is there a but?"

"Because," I whispered. "I don't know what we are yet, and I don't want to give you the wrong idea. I like talking and dancing and spending time with you but"—visions of Adam's smiling face broke through my thoughts—"but there is still a lot you don't know about me."

"Then tell me when you're ready."

"I don't know when that will be," I continued. My heart jack-hammered in my chest. How could I say what I was feeling when I didn't understand it myself? "I can't ask you to wait—"

"I want to wait."

"But being your girlfriend right now when I am trying to figure out my future and my family and if I'm truly out from under the shadow of the Spades is so much. I want to be with you but—"

"So be with me."

Frustration burst out of me like a fire hose. "Jaxson!" I cried, throwing my hands up. "Will you stop being so agreeable! I'm freaking out over here!"

He threw his head back, laughing. "Why, baby? Trust me, I have no expectations. The fact that you even let me be in the same room with you after what I did amazes me. I'm willing to accept whatever you'll give me, because I want to be with you too."

The tiniest bud of hope unfurled inside me. "You really mean that?"

"I do." Jaxson's fingers curled around my waist. "Tell me what you want, and that's how it will be."

What I want? What do I want?

"I want... to keep spending time with you."

"I'm good with that."

"I want to kiss you."

He pumped his fist. "Yes."

A giggle burst unbidden from my lips. "I want to walk down the halls with you. Dance with you. Curl into your side in the back of your car."

"Deal, deal, and deal." He grinned. "Anything else?"

I couldn't see my face, but I knew it had to be redder than a fire engine. "I want to sleep with you."

"I am *very* okay with that. You have your way with me whenever the mood strikes."

I laughed again. Why was he so good at getting me to do that? Even when I was so nervous, I was shaking.

I don't know if it was him or me who moved first, but in the next breath, our lips connected. It was a soft, slow kiss, but it brought me to the brink and then pushed me over. All of my nerve endings were alive, fizzing and sparking with electricity.

"Let's go inside," he whispered. The words were a straight shot to my core, making my pulse pick up speed.

"I'm... uh... supposed to meet Sofia."

"Tonight then." His eyes were dark with need. I read everything he wanted to do with me in his gaze, but...

"Ezra is picking me up at nine."

He placed another peck on my lips. "Tomorrow."

I chuckled softly. "We don't have to schedule it, do we? It'll happen when the time is right."

"The time is feeling plenty right now." He kissed me again and captured my lips between his teeth, making me gasp. "I want to be with you so badly, and it's no secret."

He pressed me tighter against his body, letting me feel the obvious bulge in his pants. I bit back a moan. He was seriously battering my resolve.

Maybe we do need to schedule this thing.

"How about this?" His words penetrated my fog. "Arrange a weekend pass. I have something planned for my second apology. We can spend the weekend together and whatever happens... happens."

I was nodding before he got all the words out. "Okay. Yes, yes, and yes."

Jaxson caressed my cheek before pulling me in for one more kiss. "Until then, baby."

He walked off and I floated back inside. Was there anything that could make this day better?

I hurriedly dumped my stuff, changed, and rushed to the dorm to meet Sofia. Francis Hall where the juniors were housed was smaller than the dorms we were in the year before. Four floors instead of six, reflecting how many people had left after not making the cut. It was smaller, but the rooms were no less nice. Sofia was reclining on her king-sized bed texting Zane when I walked in.

"I like what you've done in here," I admired. She had plastered posters and photos of our summer on the walls. Pops of colors brightened the place between the blue bedspread, purple lamps, and blue and purple rug.

"Thanks." She bent over the bed and sat back up holding a bag of chips. "Ready for a junk-filled afternoon?"

"More than ready." I flopped down on her bed. "But I have to tell you something, and you can't freak out."

"I'm making no promises."

"Sofia!" I cried, half-laughing.

"I will freak out if the situation demands it. Now spill."

Rolling my eyes, I gave into my fate. "Okay, fine. Jaxson is taking me out this weekend, and I'm ninety-nine point nine percent sure we're going to have sex."

"Ahhhh!"

I knew the scream was coming. What I wasn't prepared for was her to tackle me into the sheets.

"Whoa!" She collapsed on me, holding me down as I laughed.

"Are you for real?!"

"Yes, I'm for real. What do you think?"

"What do *you* think?" Sofia lay next to me and rested her head on my shoulder. "This will be your first time, and you and Jaxson have an intense history."

"I know." Thoughts of Benjamin Shea tried to force their way into my mind. I took a breath and let it out slowly, breathing past the band forming around my chest. "I'm ready, Sofia. Jaxson has done a lot he needs to make up for, but he knows that. He's changed and... it feels right."

"Then that's all that matters." She kissed my cheek. "Are you going to tell him about Adam?"

"One day, but not right now."

"Okay. It's your decision."

I twisted around and enfolded her in a hug. I didn't know where I'd be without her supporting me. "I'm ready for junk now."

She laughed. "Let's do it."

SOFIA AND I HAD SO much fun I almost didn't want to leave. It was thoughts of Ezra and those glittering obsidian eyes that finally got me out the door. Eight thirty on the dot I burst into my room and hopped in the shower.

What are we going to do tonight? How is he possibly going to give me my request of letting me in?

My heart pounded as I looked for an outfit. I was nervous and it was no wonder why. I shared my first real kiss with Ezra Lennox. I felt the stirrings of attraction as we sat together in the library, fighting to focus while he whispered in my ear. That attraction died a fiery death when the Knights told me I was just a bet.

But now I know that was a lie, so how do I feel now? How does he feel?

The sound of knocking floated up three flights of stairs as I put on my teardrop earrings. I dashed a quick swipe of lipstick across my mouth and grabbed my bag. Ezra turned to face me when I opened the door. His eyes widened slightly.

"Wow. You look amazing."

I ducked my head. "Thanks."

He looked great too, but then he always did. He wore a simple pair of jeans and a button-up shirt that didn't leave his body to the imagination. Ezra wore proper and sexy effortlessly.

"So where are we going?" I asked as I closed the door behind me. "To your dorm? Jaxson says the rules for having girls in and out don't apply to the Knights."

"I'm the only one of us that hasn't tried to break that rule." We strode side by side across the grass. "We can go there if you want, but I had somewhere else in mind—where we can have more privacy."

"Privacy is good." Then I cringed.

That all you have to say? Think of something!

"What are we going to do?"

"You said you wanted to get to know me," he replied. "I'm going to make that happen."

We rounded the corner of the main building as I thought of a response. The quad opened before us. It was beautiful at night. The soft glow of the light posts lit up the grass and the couples who gathered on it to see the stars.

Ezra didn't stop. He led me through the quad and past the junior dorm until we reached the sports complex. It wasn't until we skirted around the back that I realized where we were going.

I stopped. "You're taking me to the roof?"

"Yeah. Is that okay? I know you used to come up here."

That he knew that from when he was following me went unsaid.

"I checked it out once and I've... been coming back ever since. It's a nice spot to think."

"It is."

"Can we go up?"

I hesitated for one more moment, then I nodded. "Okay."

We kept going. Ezra held the door open for me, ever the gentleman. It had been a long time since I climbed these stairs. The last time I had been on this roof was when I was with Ryder. The night I almost fell to my death.

Trepidation slowed my steps. What would it feel like being on this roof again? How would I keep out the memories of what happened between us? The things I had shared.

Ezra walked out in front of me to open the door. My pace had slowed considerably, but a soft glow peeking through the entrance beckoned me forward. I stepped out, and gasped.

It had always been beautiful up here—covered in string lights and made cozy by the rug and couches. In the time since I had been away, it was transformed. More lights had been put up, banishing the shadowed corners. The rug, couch, and coffee table had been replaced. Gone was the old furniture. Two couches now sat looking even more comfortable, and a new coffee table with two glasses and a plate of food in the middle. Above it all was a dark canopy.

"Did you do this?"

Ezra nodded. "I told the headmaster I wanted another space after the Knight room was broken into last year. He gave me this one."

"Amazing that you can just do that." I crossed to the couch and sat down, snuggling into the cushions. "Is there no limit to what the Knights can get away with?"

"Nope," he said, a tad cheekily. Ezra bent and handed me a glass. "Grape juice," he answered when I peered curiously at the dark liquid. "And peanut butter brownies. I didn't know how long we would be out here so I got the kitchen staff to make us a snack."

"He thinks of everything." I smiled as I kicked off my shoes and pulled my feet onto the couch. "So can I know now what we are doing?"

"It's simple." Ezra sat down on my other side. "You want to know more about me, so ask. Twenty questions, and I'll answer them all honestly."

"Wait. Are you serious?" I shifted until I was facing him, sitting on my knees. "Anything?"

"Anything."

"Only twenty?"

He cracked a smile. "Twenty seemed like a nice round number."

"Oh." I bit my lip. Where did I even start? "Can you ask me questions too? We'll take turns."

"Sure." He leaned in. "And just so you know, that counts as your first question."

I swatted his shoulder as he laughed. "No, it doesn't. Don't try to cheat me, Lennox."

"First thing you'll learn about me," he said between chuckles. "I'm not above cheating to win. Jaxson's still trying to figure out how I ended up with five wild draw four cards in a pack with only four."

"So I have to watch you."

"Definitely."

A smile tugged at my lips as I leaned back. "Okay, if that was my question, it's your turn."

"Fine." Ezra's face changed before my eyes. "I saw you two together after class. Are you and Jaxson going out now?"

I blinked. Of all the questions I was expecting, none of them had been this. "Jaxson and I are... figuring things out as we go."

"So you're not exclusive?"

"It's my turn," I said softly.

"Right. Go ahead."

I didn't ask right away, taking my time to think of what I really wanted to know. "Why have I never met you before Evergreen? If you and Ryder and the Knights have been friends for so long? Other kids would come by the house when I was there, but never the three of you."

"Ryder didn't want us there." Ezra leaned over and picked up two brownies. He handed one to me. "He hated that house where his mom hid away and his shit stain of a dad roamed the halls. He preferred coming to our houses, and honestly, we didn't like going there much either. It's better now that Mr. Shea is gone... which I guess is an awful thing to say since the guy has been missing and presumed dead for over two years."

Brownie crumbles littered my skirt as my hand clenched. It was not an awful thing to say. I shoved the food in my mouth rather than reply, and Ezra took his turn.

"Are you and Jaxson exclusive?"

I choked. "No," I cried in between hacking up brownie. "We're taking it one step at a time. Why do you want to know about us?"

"Is that your next question?" I swatted him again and he laughed. "I want to know because... he's not the only one who wants to be with you."

The air whooshed out of my lungs. I gaped at him as the remainder of my brownie slipped through my fingers. "What?"

"I promised total honesty so here it is. I want to be with you. I've *always* wanted to be with you, and I fucking hated every minute of you being marked."

My head was spinning. He couldn't really be saying these things. "But you— You hated *me* for what I did to get back at you."

"I hated what you did, and I hate what my mom thinks of me, but... is it crazy that I'm even more attracted to you now." Ezra's eyes seemed even darker. Twin endless pools threatening to pull me into the abyss. "You're hardcore, Moon. Brutal. I've never met anyone like you. Willing to do whatever it takes."

"Most people don't like that quality."

"Most people aren't me."

I swallowed thickly. "I'm starting to see that."

At that moment, something passed between us that I would never understand on a conscious level. Something deep, primal... brutal... like I had tipped over into the abyss and found a darkness I knew well.

A shiver went up my spine as he gazed at me. I spoke to take my mind off the conflicting feelings.

"It's my turn," I croaked. "Tell me about your family. I don't know anything about your life outside of this school except your mom is in news."

Ezra polished off his brownie before answering. "I have an older brother."

"You do? I didn't know that."

"Most people don't. He's twenty-six, has his own life and family, and only visits at Christmas. Mom had him while she was in college and he was raised by his dad."

I picked up on something. "His dad?"

"We have different fathers." The truth poured so easily from Ezra's mouth and it amazed me. He said he would be honest, but seeing how committed he was showed how much this meant to him.

He really wants to make it up to me, and maybe... he wants more.

"Mom met my dad while she was on assignment in the Middle East. They loved each other but he didn't want to leave and she wasn't willing to stay. It ended before she found out I existed."

"Do you ever see him?"

Ezra looked away. I half expected him to call me out for skipping his turn. "No," he finally said. "He calls and sends gifts on my birthday, but we've never met in person. He's married now, and although he never said it, I get the feeling his wife doesn't want me around."

I don't know why I did it. Ezra's face gave nothing away, but deep down I knew it was right. I crawled closer to him and draped my legs over his lap. My head I rested on his shoulder. "I'm sorry."

Ezra was still for a second, then his arm wrapped around my waist. I relaxed as he put his chin on my head. "It's okay. I have Mom."

We were quiet for a moment. I wanted to get to know him, but I didn't want this night to be sad.

"How about this for a question?" I asked, abandoning the order. "What's your favorite flavor of ice cream?"

A laugh ripped from his throat like it startled him. "Ice cream? Okay. Butter pecan."

I gagged. "Ick! I would have accepted chocolate, rocky road, even mint chip, but not butter pecan."

He was full-blown laughing now. "You can't judge my answers. We're putting that in the rules."

"Too late now," I teased. "I'll give you another try. Do better this time."

"Shit. What's your favorite?"

"Dulce de leche, of course."

"If I say the same, will that be acceptable?"

"Now you're getting it."

We dissolved into laughter. The rest of the night we spent eating brownies, laughing, and talking about everything. The sun was peeking over the horizon by the time Ezra walked me back to my dorm.

I closed the door between us, then slid down it, collapsing into a puddle on the floor. A few hours ago, I thought things couldn't get better. I was wrong.

KAI PLOPPED DOWN NEXT to me. "I was up all night doing homework. What's your excuse?"

I peeled my head off the desk and stared blearily at him. "What?"

"You looked wrecked, Moon. What time did you get to bed?"

"Two hours ago." I scrubbed my eyes. "But it's okay. It was worth it."

"What did you do?"

"I hung out with a friend."

"Sofia," he stated.

I didn't bother to correct him. "Why don't we study together tonight? I still have yesterday's homework to do and they'll pile more on today."

"Nice. Come to my room. It's—"

I shook my head. "Can't. Girls can't go into boys' rooms and vice versa. That was in the handbook. Did you even crack it open?"

"I used it to kill a spider then threw it out. Does that count?"

Shaking my head, I replied, "You're going to make me work overtime at this student guide thing. Aren't you?"

His grin said it all.

Kai and I chatted while the classroom filled up. Sofia and Zane ran in, looking suspiciously disheveled, right before the AV students wheeled the television inside.

"Quiet down," Markham said. "It's time for the announcements."

No sooner had she spoke than Ezra's face filled the screen. "Good morning, junior class, and welcome to the second day of the year. We have a lot of exciting things happening this semester and I know we're all looking forward to it."

Kai snorted. "This guy is a smiley one, isn't he?"

"On camera he is," I said under my breath.

Ezra beamed back at us. "The homecoming dance is at the end of this month. Next month we have the Halloween dance, and then finally is the winter trip."

"Whoop!" Cheers went up around the room. Everyone was looking forward to having fun at Evergreen again—me included.

"—or A Night in Paris," Ezra said. "You will cast your vote for the homecoming theme at the end of the week. Now our headmaster with a few words."

I tuned out Evergreen and took out my homework. I worked until the bell rang for another day of classes.

"Winter trip sounds fun," Zane said as we gathered our things. "We never had any of that at our old school."

"It is fun if the upperclassmen are to be believed," Sofia replied. "It's also one big hookup fest so that's why everyone is excited."

"I like the sound of that." Zane threw an arm around a giggling Sofia.

"What? No chaperones?" Kai asked.

Sofia shook her head. "There are. They keep room keys so they can bust in at any time, but there are plenty of places to sneak away."

"Which you two will be doing, so it'll just be me and Val." He draped an arm on my shoulder. "We'll have fun together. You can teach me how to ski."

Something made me turn my head. Our eyes connected instantly. Jaxson looked at me, then the arm on my neck, and his eyes narrowed into slits.

"I won't be much of a teacher." I bent down to get my bag, making the hand fall off. "I have no idea how to ski. I've never even seen snow."

The four of us set off for the door. Jaxson slipped out of the classroom before I could think to catch up to him.

"There's also the homecoming dance," Sofia spoke up. "This will be Val's first time going."

"If I go." We stepped into the hallway. "I'm not sure—"

"Hello, Valentina."

I froze. I knew that voice. There was no mistaking that voice. "Isabella." I turned and there she was looking even lovelier than usual. Her hair had grown and fell in soft waves to her waist. The red dress that was our uniform looked like a fashion statement on her. Flanking her was the rest of the Diamonds: Natalie, Airi, Genesis, Cade, and Axel.

She swept her hair back and shot me a smile. "Did you have a nice summer?"

"I did." I matched her pleasant tone. "And you?"

"It was lovely. Mother and I went to Russia to see the ballet. It reminded me why the art is so superior. No one can match the hard work and dedication of a ballerina." She lifted her shoulders. "Hip-hop was a cute distraction, but that's all it was. I never took it seriously."

Nodding, I closed the distance between us. "You said something to me the night we first met. That you become the best by going up against people stronger than you and coming out on top. You said you embrace every challenge, and you know, I actually had a little respect for you after you said that."

I smirked. "That's gone now. We both know you took that competition seriously, and that you were gutted when you lost and Mommy pulled you off the team. I *beat* you, Bruno. How does it feel to lose?"

Isabella's polite mask disappeared so quickly you would have thought it was never there. She bared her teeth. "You're much more familiar with the feeling so I don't have to tell you."

"Ooh. That wasn't very nice." I snapped my fingers. "Get her for that, guys."

The Diamonds looked at me like I was nuts.

"How do I turn them on?" I asked Isabella. "I'm their leader now. Aren't they supposed to be my faithful minions?"

"You're not leading the Diamonds!"

"But that's how it works. I beat you." I was having way too much fun riling her up.

"You *did not* beat me!" Isabella was about as red as her dress. "It was a stupid contest that no one cares about. Let's see you challenge me in ballet."

A hand fell on my shoulder. "Everything okay, Moon?"

"Everything is fine," I said to Kai. "I don't have time for games this year, Isabella, and as you like to keep reminding everyone—neither do you. How about we stay out of each other's way?"

She spoke through gritted teeth. "I don't think so."

"Suit yourself." I gave her my back and walked off with my friends.

"What was that all about?" Zane asked.

"I'll let Sofia tell you about the Diamonds. She explains this craziness much better than me."

Crazy was the word the boys were both using when we walked into advanced literature. The setup in here was a bit different with tables for two instead of individual desks. My eyes swept the room for a place all four of us could sit until I landed on Ezra.

He looked from me to the spot next to him, making it clear what he wanted me to do. "Uh, guys. I'm going to sit over there." I was off before they replied, but by the footsteps behind me they were following.

Zane and Sofia took the table in front of him while Kai sat at the one behind. Ezra pulled out my chair for me to sit. "Ever the gentleman," I teased.

"You said last night you like guys who hold open doors."

"I've dealt with a lot of assholes in my life, so yes, I don't mind a nice guy."

"I wouldn't say I'm nice," he said lowly. He leaned in until I was engulfed in his piney scent. I loved the way Ezra smelled. "Hope you can settle for me."

"We'll see."

"Sorry I kept you up all night."

"What happened last night?" I sprang back so fast I almost toppled out of my seat. Jaxson stood over us, grinning away. "Why were you keeping my girl up?"

Ezra gave him a grin so wicked a flush went up my neck. "Why do you think?"

"We *talked*," I blurted. "We were up all night talking."

Ezra didn't skip a beat. "This time."

My cheeks were positively flaming. I thought it once, and I knew it now. The prim and proper Ezra was an act.

Jaxson wasn't fazed. Laughing, he went to take the seat behind us until he saw who he was sitting next to. A scowl took over both of their faces as Jaxson and Kai locked eyes.

What is up with these two?

"Jaxson, do you want to sit next to Ezra instead?"

"Nah, you're good, baby." He dropped his bag and sat down as the classroom door opened again. Confused, I looked away at the sound of someone calling for our attention.

"Good morning, class. Welcome to Advanced Literature and Composition. I am Professor Coleman." The man who stood before us was average in every way. Average height, average build, average short haircut, and average face. "Thank you for choosing your seats and pairing up with your friends." He smiled. "Now I know exactly who *not* to put you with."

Groans filled the room.

"That's right. Everyone up. You have assigned seats."

Grudgingly, I picked up my stuff and trudged to the back of the room. Coleman wasn't joking. He put Sofia and Zane on opposite sides of the room. Ezra was up two rows ahead of me. Jaxson ended up next to Maverick and Kai—

"We meet again." Kai flashed me a smile as he sat down. I had no trouble returning it. I'd much rather be with him than Natalie, Airi, or Isabella.

"Get a good look at the person next to you. They will be your partner for the rest of the year." Coleman grabbed the clicker off his desk and pulled up his slideshow. "This semester you and your partner will be working on a single project broken up into four parts. You will read the books *Night, The Diary of Anne Frank,* and *The Book Thief.* For each book, you will hand in a ten-page paper."

I gaped at him. I was wrong about this guy being average. This was top-level academic pile on.

"Your final will be a twenty-page essay and presentation on the Holocaust. You will receive only two grades this semester so failing one will mean you have no chance of achieving the semester requirement. That should properly motivate you to take this seriously." He swept a stern gaze over us like we were planning to do the opposite. "You and your partner can split the work however you like, but I expect four papers and a presentation. Understood?"

"Yes, Professor Coleman."

"Good. Then one at a time, come up and take your first book."

Kai went up first and came back with a copy of *Night* for me. "How do you want to do this?" he asked.

"Well, the first paper isn't due until the end of the month so why don't we read the book this week, and next week we'll figure out how we'll split up the paper."

"Cool."

We cracked it open and got to reading, sitting in silence until the bell rang. The rest of our classes were no easier, and we walked out with so much homework Zane and Sofia said they would come to the library to study with us.

"I can't believe I was looking forward to junior year," Sofia griped.

"You were dazzled by dances and winter cabins," I replied. "That's how they lure us in to coming back."

We stepped into Markham's class laughing. One by one, we rescued our cells out of the phone box. Mine buzzed in my palm as soon as I picked it up.

"One second, guys."

A glance at the screen brought a frown to my lips.

Unknown number?

I hit open.

555-4653: You didn't think this was over, did you?

"What?"

"Val, you coming?"

I tore my eyes away. Sofia and the boys were heading for the door. "I'll catch up."

They shrugged and walked off while I went back to the message. That was it. Just one sentence from a number I didn't recognize. A creepy sentence.

What is that supposed to mean?

I tapped in a reply.

Me: You have the wrong number.

That done, I put my phone away and hurried to catch up with my friends.

The library was just how I remembered it. Dim, cool, and filled with the whispers of flipped pages. We found a study table at the back and sat down.

"Want to start with government?" Zane asked. "We have a quiz tomorrow."

I groaned. "I forgot about that."

We pulled out our government textbooks and got to work.

"Alright," Zane began. "What were the effects of tariffs on—"

"Excuse me?"

We stopped. Standing before our table was Paisley Winters. She gave us a smile that twitched around the edges. "Do you mind if I... sit with you guys?"

Sofia frowned. "What? Why?"

She held up an identical government textbook. "I thought we could study together."

I shared a look with Sofia. Both our faces looked like they were saying "What the hell is going on?"

"Paisley," I started, "I think—"

"Are you kidding?" Our attention snapped to Kai. "Now you want to sit next to Valentina? Why, because that fucking mark was lifted?"

Paisley shrank under his fury. "I-I just—"

"That's it, isn't it? A bunch of guys tell you it's okay to act like a decent human being, and here you are."

Paisley's eyes grew dangerously bright. "I'm s-sorry, I—"

"She deserves better than you," he snarled. "Get out of here."

Face crumpling, she spun around. I quickly got to my feet.

"No, stop!" I grabbed her before she could run. "Paisley, it's okay. You can sit with us."

"Are you serious?" asked Kai.

Even Sofia looked unsure. "Val?"

"If I can forgive the Knights, then I can forgive her." Paisley's shoulders shook with tears. I rubbed them as I pulled her in for a hug. She grabbed me in a death grip as she buried her face in my neck and sobbed. "I don't want to be angry and hurt and vengeful anymore. If everyone else is willing to put the past behind them and start over, then so am I."

I sat Paisley in my seat since Kai was still scowling at her. I took the spot next to him and pulled my textbook to me. "Okay, the effects of tariffs..." I went on like nothing was different, and after a few minutes, the rest of them joined me.

My phone buzzed halfway through Zane's answer. I slid it over and pulled up the text.

555-4653: No. This is definitely the right number. That was a cute speech you gave. I'll have to do something about the not being angry and vengeful thing.

What the fuck?

I twisted around, scanning the scattered faces in the library. Everyone I saw was reading, writing, or studying. No one was on their phone.

Me: Who is this?

The reply came in seconds.

555-4653: You can call me Ace. We're going to have a lot of fun this year, Valentina Moon.

Me: No, we're not, creep. Get out of my inbox or I'll block you.

Ace: I wouldn't do that. That would piss me off, and trust me, you'll want to keep me happy.

Me: FUCK. OFF.

Ace: I know what you did last year.

The message made me pause with my finger hovering above the block button.

Ace: I know about Scarlett LeBlanc.

The breath whooshed out of my lungs like I had been punched in the gut. Those five words blurred as the phone shook in my hand.

"Valentina?"

How? Who is this?

"Valentina." A hand grabbed my wrist, making me jump. I looked into Kai's concerned eyes. "Are you okay?"

"Yes," I forced out. I dropped my phone into my lap. "I'm fine."

Chapter Five

I was not fine. I sent text after text to the mysterious Ace, but got no reply after the final message about Scarlett.

What did that mean? What did they know? Why did they say we were going to have fun together this year? And why did I have a terrible feeling that it wouldn't be fun for me?

I was in such a state by Friday, I jerked out of my skin when someone touched me.

"Whoa, baby. It's just me." Jaxson's voice soothed my nerves like water dousing a fire. I spun around and fell into his arms. "Are you okay? What's wrong?"

I shook my head. I hadn't told anyone about Ace. I didn't know what to tell them. Until I knew what I was dealing with, I was suffering in silence.

"Nothing. It's just been a long week."

He stroked my hair. "Do you still want to leave with me this weekend?"

"I want that so much it's insane."

His throat rumbled with his chuckle. "Let's not waste any more time then. My car is out front."

"I've got my stuff." I took my backpack out of my locker and slammed it shut. We turned to leave just as Sofia, Zane, and Kai strolled up.

"Hey, Moon, what are you doing tonight?" Kai planted himself in front of us. "We heard there is going to be a party down at the cliffs. Want to come?"

"I can't. I've got a weekend pass. I won't be back until Sunday."

"Where are you going?"

"Mind your business, South Africa." Jaxson took my hand and pulled me away. Sofia covertly tossed me a wink behind the boys' back.

"Why are you like that with Kai? You two have been at each other's throats since you first met."

Jaxson didn't look at me, but I could see his scowl. "I don't like that guy. He's always staring at you, following you around, and acting like he's your protector."

"He's my friend."

"He's into you," he said firmly.

I gaped at him. "No, he's not. Kai just got out of a relationship. He's still hung up on his ex-girlfriend."

"He's hung up on getting into your pants."

Rolling my eyes, I veered to the right and bumped his shoulder. "Why are you being jealous? I'm telling you, he's not into me, and I'm not into him." I grinned. "Besides, it's you I'm going away with this weekend."

I saw the corner of his mouth curl into a smile. "That is true."

Thankfully, we dropped the subject of Kai and shifted the conversation as we escaped out onto the front lawn. "What did you tell your mom to get the pass?"

"I said I was going to Sofia's this weekend. My mom is cool, but I'm not about to tell her I'm going off with a guy. What did you tell your dad?"

"I said I was going off with a girl."

"You did not!"

He laughed. "No, I said me and Ryder were going to check out a college. The guy was so happy at the idea of me and higher education that he gave permission on the spot."

We passed through the gates of the school. A lone yellow sports car sat waiting for us.

"No Clive?"

"Nah, I'm driving." Jaxson held open the door for me. I waited until he slid inside to pick up our conversation.

"Why would he be so happy about you checking out colleges? Are you not thinking of going?"

The engine purred to life under Jaxson's hands. "My plan has always been to take over for dad. College never seemed necessary."

I leaned back into the soft leather seats. I thought the nerves would hit me by now. Instead, I felt safe and comfortable. "You're lucky. You know exactly what you want to do. I wish I did."

"No, you're lucky, Val, because you can do anything. You may not know now, but when you figure out what you want, you'll make it happen. While it'll be handed to me."

Our hands moved at the same time. Jaxson laced our fingers over the console.

"Will you tell me where we're going now?"

"It's a surprise." He inclined his head. "Not that the location really matters since I'm not planning on letting you out of bed all weekend."

Thump, thump, thump.

How he could make my heart gallop up my throat with one sentence had to be some kind of gift. I couldn't believe we were doing this.

"You can get some sleep," said Jaxson. "It's a long drive."

"I won't be able to fall asleep."

I fell asleep.

When I woke a while later, the sun had set. "Jaxson?" I mumbled. I propped myself up to peer at him. At some point he had leaned my seat back. "Where are we?"

Nothing outside of my window looked familiar. Tall buildings had replaced the trees, and people-filled streets lit up by traffic lights where there was once nothing but serene nature.

"We're almost there."

I set the seat back and relaxed as the city zipped by me. I had no clue where I was, but I wasn't worried. I knew wherever we were going was somewhere I wanted to be.

Soon the buildings fell away and we turned on a single stretch of road. Hedges blocked the view on all sides for a while. I gasped when we finally got past them.

"Jaxson," I breathed.

"I said I would take you to the beach."

An endless ocean spread out before my eyes. My breath caught at the sight of the moonlight dancing on the waves. It was so beautiful.

"We have a house out here," he continued. "Own the whole stretch so it's completely private. What do you think?"

"It's perfect."

Five minutes later, a white two-story house peeked over the horizon. Jaxson pulled into the driveway while I tried to close my mouth. I needed to stop gawking at everything, but this beach house was incredible. It was all windows which must have been magnificent during the day.

Jaxson let us inside with his key. "How about a quick tour and then we'll hit the water."

Water? What about hitting the sheets?

I bit my lip to keep that thought in. I didn't want to sound too eager. I *was*, but I didn't want to sound it.

"Okay."

Jaxson took me through the rooms. "I had food delivered," he said when we were in the kitchen. "But I can't cook so don't expect too much."

I laughed. "Don't worry, I can. We won't starve."

The living room, dining room, and bathroom were next until finally we stopped in front of a door upstairs. "This is our room."

Jaxson pushed into a bedroom that was clearly his. Band posters decorated the walls, and the blue and black décor screamed him. His bed was massive. It took up nearly the entire space.

"So that's the place." He turned and shot me a grin. "Ready to go swimming?"

My eyes flicked to the bed. "I didn't bring a bathing suit."

"That's alright. I had that delivered too." Jaxson darted around his bed and bent to get something I couldn't see. When he stood, he was holding my bathing suit in his hands. "See. It's perfect."

I goggled at the wisp of fabric between his fingers. "That's not perfect; that's dental floss!"

His grin turned wicked. "That's what's perfect about it." He put it on the bed, and then pulled his trunks out of his bag. "I'll get dressed downstairs and meet you in the water."

He jogged out, leaving me with the string thong bikini.

What am I going to do with this guy? I thought as I held it up. This left nothing to the imagination.

Sighing, I got dressed and wandered downstairs. I saw Jaxson in the distance, enjoying the water as the moon cast its light upon us. He turned to me as I got close.

"Oh, come on," he whined.

I gave him a wicked grin of my own. I wore the bikini with a huge t-shirt over it.

Jaxson rose out of the water, arms out. "Get over here."

Laughing, I ran at him and leaped into his arms. Jaxson caught me and spun me around as the waves washed over us.

"Let's not go too deep," I said. "I can't swim."

"We'll stay right here."

I slid down Jaxson's body and leaned until the back of my head touched the water. Legs wrapped around his waist, he held me up as I gazed at the shimmering sky.

"Do you like it?" He began to move, slowly twisting in a circle as I trailed my hands through the water.

"I love it. Thank you for bringing me here. I needed some time away."

"First week back and things are already crazy?"

"I know about Scarlett LeBlanc."

"You have no idea."

"Then tell me. I'm listening."

I straightened and draped my arms around his neck, smiling into those shining blue eyes. "Maybe later. I have other things on my mind this weekend."

"Would those other things be... this?"

Jaxson rose up and captured my lips. The kiss ignited something in me I once thought I would never feel. All the new sensations that had been wreaking havoc on me since Jaxson first pushed my hair behind my ear.

We broke apart, panting.

Jaxson's grip on me was tight. I could feel his need through the fabric of his trunks. "We should probably go upstairs now."

I grinned. "In a minute. You wanted to mess around in the ocean so"—I smacked the water into his surprise face—"let's do it."

"That's it!"

I squealed as I scrambled off of him. What followed was the water fight to end all water fights.

"You can't win this, Moon!"

I was laughing so hard my sides ached. I darted through the wave as he lunged for me.

"I will catch you and claim my prize."

"Do it then!" No sooner had the words left my mouth than he pounced. I found myself scooped into his arms and on the receiving end of such a searing kiss I wondered what the hell I was doing in this ocean when I could be upstairs with him.

I wriggled out of his hold. "Come on, Van Zandt." I walked backward out of the water onto shore. "Claim your prize."

"Don't have to tell me twice."

Jaxson took off just as I did. I spun and ran, tearing off for the house with him hot on my heels. My wet feet smacked against the tile as I dove for the stairs. It was almost as loud as my pounding heart. Or maybe that pounding was the sound of Jaxson thundering up the stairs after me.

After all this time, everything that had happened to me, I was going to be with Jaxson Van Zandt.

I burst into the bedroom and skidded to a halt in front of the bed. Jaxson was on me the minute I turned around. We collapsed on the sheets in a laughing heap.

Jaxson rose up, straddling me, and I took the chance to rip the shirt over my head and fling it across the room. It landed with a loud splat.

I shivered under his gaze as he drank me in. "I knew I made a good choice with the bikini." He reached out and pushed my hair back. My eyes fluttered shut at his touch.

"We'll go slow, baby. Like I promised."

"Okay," I whispered. I trusted him. I should have been a mess of nerves and shakes, but I was relaxed as he slipped the top... then the bottom of the bikini off of my body. His trunks joined them on the floor and finally it was just us.

"You are so beautiful." Jaxson's hand started at my temple and then traveled down. Goose bumps were left in his wake as his finger glided over my chest and through the valley of my breasts. I hitched my breath when he reached my belly button, but his hand veered off and settled on my hip. Jaxson kissed me. Once. A chaste peck on the lips. Then one on my chin. Then he kept going.

Jaxson dropped a scorching trail of kisses leading to my breast.

"Jaxs— Oh."

A small exclamation escaped my lips. Jaxson took my nipple into his mouth, tongue flicking and licking it until he extracted more moans from me.

I couldn't breathe. My body was hot and shivering at the same time. Pressure built in my core until I was sure I would burst. This was exquisite torture.

Jaxson reached across the bed without lifting his head. His hand disappeared in the drawer of his nightstand and reemerged with a condom.

He keeps them close by. I wonder how many girls he's—

I cut that thought off at the knees. I didn't want to think of him with anyone else. All that mattered was that I was here with him now.

Jaxson's mouth found mine again. Our tongues tangled in a feverish dance.

He pulled back. "Are you read—"

"Yes," I cried breathlessly. I claimed his lips again. Over us I could hear the condom unwrapping. When Jaxson placed his hand on my thigh, I opened with no further prompting.

He swallowed my cry when he pushed inside. Then he swallowed the next, and the next as he moved, bringing me closer and closer to the edge.

Brilliance exploded in my mind as I finally tipped over. I clung to him, body spasming as I came down.

"Wow," I said hoarsely. "So that's what it's like."

WARMTH WRAPPED ME UP in its cocoon. I felt so comfortable, I didn't want to move.

Clink.

I cracked an eyelid open, peering across the pillow as Jaxson leaned over the nightstand. He smiled. "You're awake."

"I am now." I stretched out the kinks in my body. I was sore in all the right places. "Is that for me?"

Jaxson lifted the tray and set it down in front of me. "I brought you breakfast in bed."

"That's so sweet." I reached for the lid.

"I'd like to remind you," he said quickly, "I can't cook."

I lifted the lid and had to clap my hand over my mouth to cover my laugh. "Jaxson, everything on this tray is burned."

"Not everything," he protested. He picked up the glass of milk. "This is alright."

I giggled. I was so giddy not even overcooked eggs or black toast could get me down. "We can make breakfast together."

"Deal." He leaned in and kissed me. "How did you sleep?"

"Good." I shifted. "Although, we probably should have showered before hopping in bed. I've got sand in places sand shouldn't be."

"We can take that shower now." Jaxson had the tray moved and me in his arms before I could say yes. We took our time, exploring each other's bodies with sudsy hands. It was closer to lunchtime before we finally went downstairs to make breakfast.

I handed him the carton. "Crack the eggs for me."

"Yes, ma'am." I rolled my eyes at his salute. He was such a goofball but damned if I didn't think he was adorable.

Ring. Ring.

I heated the pan as the ringing behind me ceased.

"What's up, Eugene? Yeah. Why? It's all good, man. She's with me."

My ears perked up.

"I don't have to tell you where I go. We'll be back tomorrow. Whatever. Bye."

"Everything okay?" I asked when he hung up.

"Yeah. The guys were looking for you and freaked when you weren't answering your phone and Richards wouldn't tell them where you were."

"I left my phone at school," I admitted.

"Why?" Arms snaked around my waist. I leaned into him, letting his spicy scent envelop me.

"Because I wanted it to be just us this weekend."

"That's why I didn't tell them we were coming here." He kissed my cheek. "Just us."

Those two words made my heart flutter. "Why were they looking for me?"

"Ricky wanted to steal you away. He's way behind on the apologizing."

"I'll find him when I get back."

"Cool. Right now, it's all about food and sex. Not necessarily in that order."

"Which order would you like that to be in?"

I squealed as I was lifted off my feet. I barely had a chance to shut off the stove before I was whisked upstairs.

THE WEEKEND AT THE beach house was so amazing, it was hard to leave when the time came. I stayed awake for the three-hour drive back so I got to see the city disappear and be replaced by anonymous motorways, then finally the town of Evergreen.

Jaxson drove around the school to the student parking in the back. Together, we walked back to my building where he kissed me on the doorstep before leaving.

I didn't go inside right away. Instead, I headed for the main building. I had stashed my phone in my locker for the weekend. I had wanted it to be about me and Jaxson, but I also didn't want to worry about Ace.

My feet slowed as I neared my locker. I so much wanted to believe those messages were a sick joke, but then how did this person know to use Scarlett's name?

I took my phone out of my locker and it buzzed in my hand. I had unread notifications.

There were the calls I was expecting from Maverick, Ezra, and Ryder checking on me. Then there were five from a name I never wanted to see again.

Ace: I bet you're dying to know how much I know about Scarlett LeBlanc.

Ace: No answer? Are you mad at me?

Ace: Where are you? I don't see you anywhere.

Ace: Answer me, Valentina.

Ace: You took a trip off campus and left your phone behind. Tsk, tsk. Naughty, naughty. If you pull that again, you'll make me angry. I told you not to do that.

That was the psycho's final message. I was tempted to type another fuck off, but I stopped myself. Instead, I called Sofia.

"Hey, Val. Are you back?"

"Just got back."

"Then get over here *now*. I want to know everything."

"On my way."

The truth was I'd rather be grilled by Sofia than sit in my empty dorm away from everyone. Whoever this person was they were clearly keeping tabs on me. I'd feel safer with someone else around.

Sofia yanked me inside when I arrived.

"How was it? Where did you guys go?"

I flopped down on her bed. "He took me to his beach house. It was—in a word—perfect."

The mattress bounced as she joined me. "I'm so happy for you, Val. You gave me and Zane the idea to sneak away next weekend. His parents are going out of town so if we can get passes, we'll have the place to ourselves." She heaved a sigh. "This whole cameras in the staircase thing is really putting a crimp in my sex life."

"Shameless," I teased. We laughed and my tension started to ease. "How was the party?"

"It was one big booze-filled make-out session." She nudged me with her foot. "Some interesting things did happen. Kai heard Natalie running her mouth about you and he went off. She clammed up quick."

"He did? He doesn't have to do that."

She hummed. "Also, Eric came up to me at the party looking for you."

"For me? What did he want?"

"He didn't say. Just told me to tell you he wants to talk."

That was weird, but I pushed it aside for the moment. "Let's just chill today, okay? I want to keep ignoring the mountain of homework I have waiting for me."

Sofia was happy to comply and we spent the rest of the afternoon eating and hanging out. My mood had lifted by the time I left the junior dorm. I crossed the quad with a smile on my face, thinking of my weekend with Jaxson.

Buzz. Buzz.

The smile melted away. I hoped it wasn't them; I wanted to hold on to my happiness for longer.

1 Unread Message: Ace

Ace: Good. You're back.

I halted. Looking around, I saw plenty of people in the quad with their phones. None of them were paying particular attention to me, but I took note of every face—both familiar and unfamiliar.

Ace: Good. You're back. So now I can tell you about the rules. They are very simple so even you should have no trouble following them. One: Keep your phone on you. If it's not in the phone box; it's on your body. Two: You don't tell anyone about

me. **Three: Do everything I say or people will find out about Scarlett LeBlanc.**

Anger surged through me and I typed my reply.

Me: You don't know anything about Scarlett, and I am not doing a thing you say. So again: Fuck off.

I took one step and the reply came back right away.

Ace: So you need proof. That's fine. I'm happy to provide.

My face screwed up in a frown. Proof? What proof could they possibly have?

Another notification popped up on my screen, this time telling me of a media message. I clicked it without a thought.

A blur of colors appeared on my screen. I could make out nothing as the camera shook.

What is this?

A scream tore from my speakers and I almost dropped the phone. The picture became clear as I righted my cell and dread like I had never felt before turned me to lead.

I watched myself on the screen. I saw me scream and fight as Scarlett LeBlanc dragged me to the edge of the cliff. The cry that had been tormenting me in my dreams poured out of the speaker, and then I was there.

"Give me the phone!"

"If you want the fucking thing so bad then have it!"

I threw it. The phone crested high over our heads and Scarlett's head snapped back as she followed its flight. She jumped, straining to reach it, and... missed.

The phone soared over the edge of the cliff and Scarlett went with it. Her screams echoed through the clearing until I could hear them no more.

My hands shook as the screen went black.

Then the phone buzzed with another message, and I ran. I ran through the quad to my dorm without pausing for breath. My front door flew open with a bang that rattled the building.

How? How?! How could they have that video? Who could have seen?

I tore into my room, then locked and bolted every door and window. I felt exposed. Unseen eyes crawled all over my skin until it was everything I could do not to claw it off.

I didn't want to. My finger slipped on the scanner three times, but things were different now. There would be no more ignoring Ace. I opened the final message.

Ace: I'm glad we understand each other now. I said we were going to have fun this year. I can't wait.

Chapter Six

"Val? Val? Val!"

My head snapped up and Kai's face came into focus. "What?"

"You what. You've been zoned out all day. You didn't even notice the bell rang *two* minutes ago."

"Shit!" I scrambled to get my things. Kai and I booked it out of the empty classroom.

Monday had dawned early, but not bright. At least not for me. I stayed up all night worrying about the video, Ace, and what I should do. More than that, I wondered what Ace was going to make me do. How was I going to get out of this?

"Why didn't you go without me?" I huffed.

Our leather soles scuffed the marble floors, making faint squeaks as we went. Kai shrugged mid-run. "I wasn't going to let you be late to orchestra. The guy is nuts."

"The guy" shot us the foulest look when we flew in seconds before the final bell.

"Miss Moon. Mr. Thomas. Do not cut it so close next time!"

"Yes, Professor Felton," we mumbled.

"Sit! Sit! Sit!" Felton punctuated every shout with a whack of his baton. The weedy, white-haired man had led world-famous orchestras for decades, but now he was the slightly deaf, ill-tempered

professor who never put down his baton and gave detention to anyone who was late.

I collected more nasty looks as I headed down the rows for
my seat. The orchestra classroom was quite impressive. It was like
a mini auditorium with Felton in the middle and us surrounding
him with instruments the school had spared no expense on. I liked
learning to play the bongos. I even liked Felton most days. What
I didn't like were the poisonous looks Isabella, Natalie, and Airi
threw me from their seats in front of me.

"Stupid bitch," Airi hissed. "Why do you bother to show up?
All you do is make a racket with those things."

I ignored her as I got out my bongos. Airi was particularly
awful to me in this class. I'm guessing having to play her replace-
ment violin made her extra prickly. But whatever her problem was,
I didn't have time for it. I had much bigger issues than scores I had
settled a year ago. Airi would have to get over it.

"Attention! Attention!" We were already silent and waiting for
his signal. "Now! Begin!"

Somehow, I made it through class and only got yelled at once.
Sofia and the twins fell in beside me as I trudged to class.

"Something is up with Val," Kai announced.

I shoved his shoulder. "No, it's not. I'm fine."

"Kai worries about you," Sofia spoke up. "And so do I. You have
been acting weird today."

"No one is being weird. No one needs to worry." I was proud of
myself for how convincingly I said that. "Let's just get some lunch.
I'm starved."

We strode into the cafeteria and joined the line. From the
smells wafting from the kitchen, I knew it would be good.

Someone tapped my shoulder.

"Don't even think of touching my dessert," I said. "I'll come out forks swinging."

"Thanks for the warning."

I blinked. That amused voice was definitely not Sofia. "Maverick?" I turned but my eyes only confirmed it. Standing before me was a wall of pecs. I traveled higher and landed on his smile.

"Valentina." He gestured with his chin. "After you get your lunch, will you come with me?"

"Where?"

The question should have come from my lips, but Kai beat me to it. Maverick glanced at him.

"Do I know you?"

"What's up, Maverick?" I asked, drawing the attention back to me.

The taller boy's muscles flexed as he shoved his hands in his pockets. I never thought of myself as someone obsessed with looks, but I couldn't help but drink him in every time I saw him.

"I have something for you," he said. "I would have given it to you sooner, but Jaxson claimed you for the weekend."

I warmed at his word choice.

"It's in the Knight room. Come with me?"

"Okay."

Maverick drifted off to the side to wait while I got my lunch—and the third degree from my friends.

"What do you think he wants to give you?" Sofia asked, eyes shining. "Ooh, I love this twelve labors thing. I wish a guy would do something like that to show how much he cares about me. Let alone four guys."

The twins spoke at the same time.

"Twelve labors?"

"What do you want me to do?"

Sofia rose up and kissed Zane's cheek. "Not you specifically, babe. The Knights acted like awful shits to Val in freshman year and now they are each doing three things to make it up to her."

"Sofia!" I cried. "Let's just tell the whole school, shall we?"

"Is it a secret? Why? It's the sweetest thing ever."

Zane captured her chin between his fingers. "Well, if you think it's sweet; sign me up."

They dissolved into giggling and flirting and I looked away. Kai sidled up to me as the lunch staff handed me a tray.

"Is she for real?"

"She added a bit more spice, but yes. The Knights are working to apologize to me."

"So that's why they're all over you all the time."

"I wouldn't... say that they were," I said under my breath. "Anyway, I've got to go. See you after lunch."

I walked up to Maverick and we left together. "Can I get a hint about this gift?"

"Nope," he replied.

"You guys know you don't have to take me places or buy me things, right? I just want to know that you're really sorry."

A hand on my arm pulled me up short. Maverick turned me to face him. "We are. *I* am. You don't know—" His voice hitched and for a moment the calm and collected Maverick vanished. It was hard seeing the naked pain on his face. "Ezra and Jaxson didn't know why you were marked, but I did. I knew Scarlett was behind it, and I fucking hated myself for doing what she wanted.

"It was wrong you being at the mercy of that monster when the one wearing that mark should have been her. But I didn't know how to stop her without telling everyone that— that she—"

"It's okay," I whispered, "I understand."

"You shouldn't!"

I stepped back at the shout. There was a battle warring inside of him, and the toll it was taking had been well hidden.

"You shouldn't be understanding, Valentina. You shouldn't be nice to me. You shouldn't forgive me. I'm the worst coward. Every day I wanted to go into administration and tell them the truth about what Scarlett did to me... and every day I couldn't do it." He tossed his head. "In the end, I figured the only way I could protect you was to give in. If I helped get you out of the school, she couldn't hurt you anymore."

It was awkward with the tray between us. Still, I stepped as close to him as I could. "Maverick, I get it now. Infecting my computer was wrong, but I'm here. You can believe me when I say I understand how you felt." I looked deep in his eyes. "I understand more than anyone ever could."

A flicker of surprise flashed in Maverick's eyes, gone as quickly as it came. As we gazed at each other, something passed between us that neither of us needed to put into words. I knew in that moment that we understood each other.

I was the first to step away. "We should go. I'm excited to see what you have for me."

"Okay." Maverick reached out and grabbed my tray. "Let me hold that for you."

Silently, we walked through the halls to the Knight room. When we rounded the corner, I saw the doorknob had been replaced with one larger and heavy duty. Maverick pulled a key from his blazer and let me in.

"It'll never change in here, will it?" I looked around at the usual toys and gadgets. "You just get more stuff, not new stuff."

He chuckled as he set my food on the table. The act made his clothes ride up, exposing a peek of toned bronze flesh. "You know, I never told the guys about your lunchtime visits."

"Really? Why not?"

He shrugged. The barest smile tugged at his lips. "I kind of like it being our little secret."

Memories of what we did the day he found out my "secret" flooded my mind. A sudden thought occurred to me.

Is that my gift? Did he bring me here for a repeat? His hands slipping under my skirt to fondle my—

"You can sit down and eat." Maverick ripped me out of my fantasy. He was seated, and peering at me while I stood in front of the door like a dummy.

"What about your lunch?" I sank down onto the cushion as he got to his feet again.

"I hate eggplant." Maverick walked around the couch and I heard shuffling behind me.

"Huh." I looked down at my eggplant parmesan. "I didn't know that. Something else to file under Maverick."

"You still keeping a file on me?"

"I have to until I have you all figured out. I'm almost there."

"You think so?" I could hear he was amused.

"Yep." I speared a piece of my food and popped it in my mouth. "You do the strong, silent sexy type well, but it turns out you're not as mysterious as you think."

He hummed. "Then I guess I can file something else under you too."

"What?"

His reply burrowed in my ear and made my heart pick up speed. "You think I'm sexy."

"That's not what you should have taken away from that comment," I shot back, face warm.

Maverick's laughter was deep and rich. I remembered how much I loved that sound. Love it for how rare it was to hear.

"If you don't want eggplant, why don't you have my garlic bread? Or the muffin?"

"You said you'd come out fork swinging if I touched that muffin." His voice grew closer as he approached the couch. "I better not risk it."

I couldn't stop a laugh even as I rolled my eyes.

"Here. This is for you."

The fork stopped halfway to my lips as I laid eyes on the present in his hand. It was a large, rectangular gift wrapped in bright green paper and a blue ribbon.

"Maverick, I— I said you didn't have to give me gifts."

"This one I do." He stepped closer. "Take it, Val. Please."

I hesitated another second. *If it's too much, you can give it back. Let him know it was the thought that counted.*

I moved my lunch to the table and let him place the gift in my lap. The wrapping fell to the floor in shreds as I revealed what Maverick had given me.

"A laptop?" I rested my palm on the shiny black cover. I didn't know much about these things and still I could tell it was expensive.

"It's to replace the one I ruined," he explained. "It's the newest model from Maverick Technologies and I had Dad upgrade it himself. Not even I could hack into this computer." Maverick opened it up. "It's pretty cool actually. He installed a malware defense he designed himself that will..."

Maverick launched into a bunch of computer stuff I didn't understand for a minute. My eyes traced his face.

He looks so happy talking about this stuff.

Abruptly, his smile melted away. "Sorry. You're not interested in the tech."

"No, I am," I protested. "I especially like how excited you get talking about it. You'll have to teach me what all of this means."

"You really want to learn?"

I bumped his shoulder and took my time pulling back. "I do."

His smile was so cute for how genuine it was. "Does that mean you'll keep it?"

"You do owe me a new one." I clutched it to my chest. "So yes, I'll keep it."

"I do owe you which is why this doesn't count as my apology."

"What?" I stared up at him as he rose again. "This is great, you don't have to give me anything else."

"Yes, I do."

"No, honestly." I twisted to track him as he went around the chair and knelt in front of a cabinet. "This is perfect."

"Trust me, Val. Just one more."

"Well, what is—" Maverick turned and nestled on his palm was something green and tiny. "What's this?" I asked, lips curling into a grin. "It's so cute."

"It's a robot. I made it myself." Maverick joined me on the couch. "She can't do much other than walk, but I thought you might like it."

"I love it." She was a small bot with flat feet and a cube head, but Maverick had painted a smiling face on it and granted her a green body. "You made this? That's amazing. The only thing I know how to make is a mess."

He tossed his head back laughing. I loved that I could get him to do that. "You have your own talents. You're the best dancer in this school while I can't handle the electric slide."

"If you teach me about this"—I held out my robot—"then I can teach you to dance."

A smile played at his lips. "You're on, Moon. But let's be clear; those are private dance lessons. No one sees me but you."

"I could live with that."

I gazed at him, and once again I felt a silent communication pass between us. I was highly aware of how alone we were right now.

"Val?"

"Yes?"

"What are you thinking right now?"

I couldn't tell him the truth. That I was wondering if the power and sex appeal his body exuded in uniform would be the same when he was out of it. My core throbbed at the very idea and I swallowed hard. One weekend of sex and now it was all I could think about.

"Nothing," I rasped. "You?"

"I'm thinking of the last time we were alone in here together."

My pulse quickened. I forced a laugh to cover my reaction. "You mean when you caught me munching on a carrot sandwich?"

Maverick shifted until he faced me. "I mean when we kissed on this couch and I had to fight every urge not to do more."

Heat surged through me like wildfire. *Okay, so we are going with honesty today.*

"Oh, yeah... that might have crossed my mind too."

Maverick came closer, scooting in until he bumped my hand and knocked my little robot over onto my palm. Maverick's hand closed over both.

"Jaxson says that you aren't boyfriend and girlfriend."

"No," I said softly. My eyes were fixed on our hands. The robot fell in my lap as Maverick laced our fingers together. "How did that come up? You guys sit around talking about me?"

Maverick's fingers slipped out of my grasp. His touch was featherlight as he traced slow circles on my arm, but goose bumps erupted all the same. I couldn't tell what he was thinking now.

"We do when Ezra announces that he's going after you with everything he's got."

My mouth fell slightly open. "He said that?" The tiniest thrill snaked through my body. More nights in Ezra's arms eating brownies and talking.

"He did, and that's why I'm saying now"—Maverick closed the distance between us until his forehead rested on me—"I'm going after you too."

His hand found mine again and brought it to his lips. "I know I don't deserve you." His breath ghosted over me. "I have no right to even think about being with you after everything I've done, but I want you so bad I can't help it."

"Maverick," I whispered. I traced my finger along his lips, heart singing with every word. "But what about Jaxson and Ezra? You guys are friends; I don't want to come between you."

He shook his head. "We'll always be friends. That won't change. We also know we can't expect more than you're willing to give us. I can share you, Valentina... as long as I have any part of you. That's enough for me."

Maverick's eyes flicked down to my lips and once again I read his mind.

"Kiss me."

Our lips collided in a spark of heat that curled my toes. I was flying again. My body bounding, twisting, and riding on a roller coaster of emotions I couldn't control.

Maverick gently pushed me down onto the couch and I wrapped my legs around his waist, completely giving myself over to the kiss. We were breathing hard when we broke apart. Maverick gazed down at me through heavy-lidded eyes.

"Is that a yes?"

I laughed. "That's definitely a yes, but if it didn't come through clear the first time, I can try again."

"Just for clarity, we should try again."

Maverick swallowed my giggle in another kiss. My food was abandoned as we spent our time on that couch, locked in each other's arms.

As the end of lunch neared, we found ourselves stretched out on the cushions, my head resting on his chest.

"Maverick?"

His hand was under my dress, tracing a design on my thighs that made me shiver. I wanted him to keep going, searching, but the bell would be calling us away too soon.

"Yes?"

"Have you...?" I trailed off, not knowing how to say this. Unease began creeping in, chasing away my happiness. "Have you been getting texts?"

"Texts? What do you mean?" His hand drifted lower until he was caressing my ass.

My breath caught. That hand was seriously distracting me. "Have you been getting texts from an unknown number? Weird ones?"

"No. Why?" His hand stilled. "Have you?"

"No," I said quickly. "Not me. One of my friends is. It seems someone in the school got their hands on their number and is now bothering them. Just wondered if they were doing it to anyone else."

"Oh." Maverick resumed his activities. "They might be, but I haven't gotten anything. Some assholes like to scam numbers and harass people, but I bet they know better than to pull that on a Knight. Is it Sofia? Tell her to come to me and I'll show her how to block unknown numbers."

I wish it was as simple as blocking Ace, I thought as my fist clenched over his chest.

"It's not Sofia," I corrected. I didn't want Maverick going to her himself and getting her curious. "But they have tried blocking them and it won't work." I lifted my head to meet his eyes. "Is there a way to trace it? Find out who owns the phone so they can get them to back off."

"Yeah, you can do that. Send them to me and I'll sort it out."

Smiling, I stretched and landed a peck on his lips. "Thank you."

Maverick's reply was to tangle his free hand in my hair and pull me in. I moaned when he nipped at my bottom lip. He played the shy and introverted game so well, but deep down there was more to Maverick Beaumont.

The hand that had been teasing me to distraction moved up to my waist, then slid beneath the lining of my panties.

Click.

"—telling you guys," Ezra's voice sounded in the room. "If we don't handle this now— Oh. Are we interrupting something?"

I scrambled off of Maverick like he caught fire. Cheeks flaming, I yanked down my dress as he pulled his hand back. Maverick's movements were much more relaxed as the Knights filed in. He sat up, straightened his tie, and put his arm around my shoulder as though it was nothing.

Jaxson grinned at us. "I see y'all have been up to some serious *apologizing* in here." The suggestion in his tone was so blatant he might as well have come out and said it. It surprised me a little. He, and Maverick, told me that they would be cool with sharing me, but still, it was odd to see my goofball act so mature about this when only a few days ago I was tangled in bed with him.

I glanced at the other Knights and saw what I expected to see. Ezra's face gave nothing away—his disguise of politeness firmly in place. As for Ryder, the mask he wore was gorgeous in its sculpted beauty, but it was expressionless.

Jaxson strode up to me and boldly claimed a kiss, unheeding of who was watching. "It's always good to see you, baby," he said when he pulled back, "but you're about to be late for class."

My eyes widened. "Shit!" Shooting out of Maverick's hold, I tossed a hasty goodbye over my shoulder and raced out the door.

My heart pounded as I booked it to class and not just for the run. I had three hot, smart, talented guys after my attention and a nutcase blackmailing me. I don't know which one of those scared me more.

Chapter Seven

"I'm so excited."

I tossed Sofia a look. "I can tell. You're practically bouncing out of your seat."

Paisley chuckled from our other side. "She's going to the homecoming dance with one of the hottest guys in school. I'd be bouncing too... on his lap."

"Paisley!" Sofia leaned over me to swat her friend. "You're so bad. Besides," she said as she straightened. "That comes after the dance."

They collapsed into giggles while I tried not to roll my eyes at my crude friends. They were giddy—everyone was. The homecoming dance was tomorrow night and we were piling on the bus to get our dresses and tuxes.

In the last few weeks, it had been like a fog lifted. Freshman and sophomore year had been nasty with pranks, bullying, sniping, fighting, revenge, and school-wide retribution handed down by the headmaster. With the mark gone, everyone could breathe again. We could have fun again.

The taunts stopped. There were no more hissed insults in the halls. No comments on my body. No insinuations that people paid me for sex. No more attempts on my life. Life at Evergreen had gone back to the way it was, and through it all, I did not receive another text from Ace.

"What kind of dresses are you getting?" Paisley asked. Things would always be a little weird between us, but I had let go of my anger toward her. I'd never be as close to her as Sofia, but I could handle a day of laughing and shopping together. "I don't really know what to wear for A Night in Paris. I wish Artic Paradise had won."

"I heard the Diamonds are pressing the headmaster to send them to Paris over spring break," said Sofia. "They got everyone to vote for this theme as a less-than-subtle hint."

I made a face. "Send to Paris? For what?"

Sofia poked her head over the bus seat to make sure no one was listening, then she gestured for Paisley to come closer. The other girl squeezed in next to me, sharing our two-person seat, as she spoke.

"I heard she's trying to elevate the status of the Diamonds," Sofia continued. "Make them as important and official as the Knights. Best in academics, best in art, best in music, all of it. They'll be known as the best in and out of the school and have say over their specific areas."

"Say over their areas?" I repeated. "As in dance? What kind of say does Isabella want?"

She gave me a look that said it all before she opened her mouth. "She wants classical dance in, and everything else out."

"My goodness that girl doesn't quit. Evergreen can't go along with this."

"Who knows what he's going to do. The Diamonds bring in a lot of great press and attention for the academy whenever Axel smashes another track record or the art world praises Genesis for her sculptures." She shook her head. "You know Evergreen is all about the school looking good."

"That is sadly true." I leaned my head back, sighing. A lot had gotten better since school started, but one thing that hasn't changed was the Diamonds' hatred of me, especially Natalie, Isabella, and Airi. Those three would hate me until I was in the grave and beyond.

The bus rumbled to the entrance of the Evergreen Promenade and we pushed the Diamonds from our minds. We had a rare afternoon out of the academy; we were going to enjoy it.

"Let's go to Maxfield," Sofia announced as we climbed out. "They hooked us up last time."

"Sounds good," said Paisley. "They have a dress I was eyeing online last night."

"Sofia! Val!"

We looked across to the second bus as the twins stepped down.

"You girls weren't serious about ditching us, were you?" Zane asked.

"Yes, I am." Sofia's voice was firm even while she threw her arms around his neck. "I don't want you to see my dress until tomorrow."

"What does that have to do with me?" Kai piped up.

"You'll tell him what it looks like."

"Why would I do that?"

Sofia snorted. "Because you're trouble, Kai Thomas."

Grinning, he winked at her. "Can't deny that." Kai moved over to me and put his arm on my shoulder. "Val will hang out with us. Won't you?"

"I could. I've already got my dress, but Sofia booked me for the afternoon."

"That's right." She linked arms with me and pulled me away. "You can't have my best friend. You'll have to settle for your brother."

He heaved a sigh like he couldn't think of anything worse. "Fine. I'll have to steal Valentina away tomorrow night."

The boys loped off. Paisley grabbed me the moment they were out of earshot.

"You're so lucky, Val."

"Me? Why?"

"Kai is so cute."

I blinked at her. "Okay."

"I can't believe he hasn't asked you to the dance yet. It's obvious he wants to."

"He— He does not!"

Sofia shook her head. "Don't go there, Paisley. Val is in deep denial that Kai likes her. Besides, she's got her hands full with the suitors she does acknowledge."

"Tell me about it. Maverick Beaumont, Ezra Lennox, *and* Jaxson Van Zandt on her tail. Did I mention how lucky she was?"

"I bet that tail is pretty sore," Sofia shot back and they howled.

"You guys are the worst," I grumbled under my breath.

"Nope. You love me." Sofia planted a kiss on my cheek. "Now let's go. There's the cutest restaurant near Maxfield. We can eat there after we shop."

Our band made it three steps before another group stepped into our path. The six of us locked eyes.

"Hey, guys." Eric favored us with a smile. "If it's cool, we were wondering if you'd want to hook up for the day."

Claire and Ciara stepped forward. "Now that we can put all the other stuff behind us," said Claire, "it would be nice to hang out like we used to."

Claire, Eric, and Ciara had formed their own threesome since Paisley came back to us. We had been civil to each other, but no one had forgotten what Eric and Claire said minutes before the Knights lifted the mark. Awkwardness hung in the air between us like a bad smell.

Sofia glanced at me. "It's up to you, Val. What do you think?"

I considered them for a while. *I'm not interested in grudges or drama anymore. Things have been good. I want to keep it that way.*

"Okay. You can come with us."

The three of them fell in step beside us as we headed for the dress shop. Maxfield was just how I remembered it—wall-to-wall clothes that cost more than my mom's rent and a cozy sitting area in the middle of the store. Eric, Ciara, Claire and I sat while the other girls looked around.

"You're not going to look for a dress, Val?" Eric asked. He bent over to pour himself a cup of tea. He held up one for me.

"No, thanks. And, no. I have my dress already. I ordered it last week."

"I ordered mine too," Claire spoke up. "The shops around here are too expensive so I went online. I think the one I got is cute."

"It *is* cute," Ciara said. "Ethan is going to love you in it."

Claire sunk into the couch, red staining her cheeks. Ethan was a junior, second in our class behind Cade, and apparently responsible for the smile on Claire's face.

"Are you two going out now?" I asked.

"Yes," said Eric.

"No!" If anything, Claire got redder. "It's just a dance. Neither of us has time for dating. We're both trying to get into Ivy League schools."

Eric shook his head. "There's always time for sex."

Claire shoved him and he almost spilled his tea, he was laughing so hard. I held back from joining in on the banter. I wasn't a part of this group.

"How about you, Val?" Eric turned to me. "Who are you going to homecoming with?"

"No one. I'm going solo."

His brows snapped together. "Really? But I heard—"

It was Ciara who swatted his shoulder this time.

"What? What did you hear?"

He shrugged. "I heard there were plenty of guys who wanted to ask you."

I looked away. I did have a few asks—three to be exact. But I told Ezra, Maverick, and Jaxson that I couldn't possibly pick one of them...

When I wanted to go with all of them. I sighed as that thought passed through my mind. I assumed keeping things casual would make it easier and give me time to sort through my feelings, but if anything, I felt more mixed up than ever.

I was addicted to all of them for so many different reasons. The way Jaxson made me laugh and kissed me until I couldn't breathe. Or curling up with Maverick with my head on his chest while his heart beat in my ear. Or sitting with Ezra on the roof while we talked about things we couldn't tell anyone else.

They hadn't pressured me or pushed for more. They had actually been great about it when I turned down their individual offers to the dance, but something was building inside of me. More and more, the sense was overwhelming me that the time would come when I would have to make a choice.

But what would that choice be?

"What do you guys think?"

I shook free of my tumultuous thoughts as Sofia and Paisley emerged from the dressing rooms to show off their choices. I joined in the oohing and aahing and focused my attention on our day of fun.

It turned out to be a good time after all. After everyone got their dresses and Eric his tux, we went to dinner at the place Sofia liked. I scarfed down the most delicious prime rib with herb sauce.

"You guys are going to have to roll me out of here." I pushed away my empty plate. "I'm stuffed."

"Dude, I'll be rolling with you." Eric plucked two mints off the table and handed me one. "My tux won't fit now. Know anyone who can do last-minute alterations?"

"They'll be busy letting my dress out."

We cracked up, and for a minute it felt like old times.

"We should go, guys," Ciara piped up. "Markham said eight o'clock."

Sofia paid the bill ignoring our protests, then we headed out. The sun had set on the promenade. Old-timey lamp posts lit our way to the buses and the waiting Professor Markham. We fell into an easy conversation as we passed through the entrance.

"There's a party at the cliffs after the dance," Paisley told me. "I heard a few of the juniors got weekend passes so they'll be able to sneak in booze."

"I might skip out on that."

"Why? It will be..." Paisley trailed off as her eyes fell on something ahead of us. "Maybe he will change your mind."

"What? Who?"

I took my attention off her to see Jaxson propped up against the bus. I let Paisley go ahead as Jaxson peeled himself off and walked up to me. He smiled that smile that turned my knees to jelly

"Hey, baby." Jaxson pushed the hair behind my ear before cupping my cheek. "I was hoping to catch up with you while we were out." His thumb caressed my lips. "I'll have to come by your place tonight instead."

"Sounds good to me."

"And tomorrow night..."

I held my breath. *Is he going to ask me to the dance again? It was hard enough saying no the first time.*

"...save me a dance."

My lips quirked up in a smile. "Are you asking me or telling me?"

He winked. "You pick. The result will be the same." Jaxson kissed me then strode off to the other bus.

"Val, we're leaving." Kai waved at me from the steps of the bus.

"Coming." I spared Jaxson one last glance before jogging up to him. "Did you find a tux?"

Kai shook his head. "Nothing I liked so I'm having Mom bring one over from home."

"Okay, I—"

Buzz. Buzz.

"One second." I fished my phone out of my pocket and glanced at the screen.

Ace.

I lurched to a stop, staring at those three letters. *Why now? What do they want?*

"Val, you okay?"

I tore my eyes up and looked into Kai's concerned face.

"I'm fine," I rasped. I dropped the phone to my side. "It's cool. Go ahead."

Kai turned his back and I chanced the opportunity to open the message.

Ace: Hope you didn't miss me.

My reply was quick.

Me: Who are you? What do you want?

Ace: Right now, I want to know how you got Jaxson Van Zandt eating out of the palm of your hand. You must be wicked good in bed, but then I wouldn't expect anything else from a pro.

Me: Fuck you.

Ace: LOL. You're tough. Maybe that's what he likes about you. As much as he likes playing with your hair.

Me: Just tell me what you want! What will it take for you to delete that video?

Ace: I'll tell you what it will take...

The next reply made my eyes widen. The phone shook in my hands as I typed my response.

Me: You can't be serious! I'm not doing that!

Ace: If you don't, I'm sending this little video to the police. Try me. It'll be just as fun seeing you hauled in for questioning.

"Hey!"

I jerked. The phone went sailing out of my hand.

"Get out of the way, Moon," Airi snapped. "People are trying to get on."

Kai bent to pick up the cell at his feet. I dove for it, snatching it up before his fingers could close over it. He gave me a crazy look. "Val? What's up with you?"

"Nothing." I shoved the phone in my pocket. "Everything's fine." I picked myself up and scurried off. Paisley and Sofia waited in the back for me. They happily chatted away as I took my seat, their minds on beautiful gowns and handsome dates. A thought penetrated my mind and flooded me with an awful certainty. These weeks of carefree fun were over.

Ace was going to make my life hell.

"IT'S NICE TO HEAR FROM you again," a smooth, and distinctly female, voice sounded in my ear. "I had fun working for you last year. I'm guessing you have more interesting projects for me."

I paced the length of my room, breathing deep to slow my racing heart. I was surprised Alex had picked up the phone. We had spoken only through text when my hired hacker helped me get my revenge.

"I need your help," I announced. I wasn't beating around the bush. "Someone is blackmailing me and I don't know who. If I give you a phone number, can you do anything with that?"

"I can do a lot with that."

"Perfect. I'll send you the number right now."

"My standard rates apply."

"Money isn't an issue." I stopped pacing and sat on my bed. "I'll pay anything. I just need this to stop."

"I'll text you the amount. Pay within the hour."

"Fine." I fell back onto the comforter. "Oh, and can I know your name now?"

"No."

Click.

Sighing, I let the phone fall from my hand. I couldn't blame "Alex" for her secrecy. She was smart. Maybe if I had been, I wouldn't have gotten into this mess.

Someone else had been in the woods that day, watching us, filming us, and we never knew.

People know about the cliffs. Anyone could have been out there. I was so stupid to suggest meeting up there after Scarlett. I was even more idiotic to not realize she was following me.

Stop, another voice countered. *Beating yourself up won't change anything. I just have to hope Alex comes through for me.*

A knock from downstairs shook me from my thoughts. I went down to let Jaxson in.

"Hey." He enfolded me into a hug and I buried my face in his chest. I must have held on too long because he pulled back, the grin missing as he looked down at me. "Are you alright?"

"Yes, I'm just glad you're here. Let's go up."

Jaxson caught me halfway up the stairs and lifted me into his arms. I laughed as he raced me to my room and made short work of undressing me. I loved sleeping with Jaxson. I felt relaxed and comfortable with him like I hoped I would when the time came to be with someone.

We faced each other that night, noses brushing as we gazed across the pillows.

"Are you sure you're okay?" Jaxson tangled his fingers in my hair; it didn't bring the usual surge of happiness. "You've been acting strange for a while."

I don't give this guy credit. He's way more perceptive than I thought.

I chewed my lip, considering what to share. "It's been a weird few weeks. Sometimes I feel like I'll never really get out from under the mark."

His hand stilled. "What do you mean? Have people been messing with you?"

"No. If you don't count the usual from the Diamonds. It's just... how do we know everything that happened last year is really over?"

"You're talking about Scarlett." Jaxson propped himself up. The blankets fell down to his waist, drawing my eyes away from the look on his face. "Val, that is over. She's dead. She can't hurt anyone anymore." There was a hardness in his voice that came about specifically when Scarlett was brought up.

"That doesn't mean this is over. Someone could find out that there is more to her being gone." I picked myself up to look him in the eye. "There could be more Spades."

"If there were, we would know by now. They would have acted after we told everyone the mark was gone, but there's been nothing."

I studied him. "You really haven't heard anything? No notes? No cards? No rumors?" I took a breath. "No texts?"

"Nothing." Jaxson grasped my shoulders. "Baby, it's over."

I let him gather me in his arms, saying nothing.

I didn't know what it meant that Ace was only targeting me and apparently leaving the Knights alone, but I did know one thing: this was not over.

"VAL, WHAT DO YOU THINK?"

"You look amazing. Zane is going to be drooling."

Sofia twirled in front of my vanity, grinning away. "That's the idea."

The dress she had chosen was perfect—a pretty pale pink with a tight bodice and a skirt that flared at her waist. It rose above her knees as she spun. We were getting ready for the dance in my dorm.

Or at least, Sofia was getting ready. I was in my bathrobe lying on my bed.

"We're going to the party afterward," she continued. "Please say you're coming. I heard the Knights will be there."

I stood and joined her at the vanity. I reached for my lipstick while she dug through my earrings. "Why does everyone think that will convince me? I don't have to be everywhere they are."

Sofia lifted her brow at my reflection. "Four smoking hot guys competing for your attention. Why *wouldn't* you be wherever they are?"

I might have laughed if it wasn't for one word. "Three guys, Sof. Not four." I bent my head until our gaze broke. "Ryder has not been after my attention."

She was quiet for a moment. "What's going on there? I thought things were better between you two."

"I thought so too. He hasn't been mean or cold or anything. He says hi when he sees me, and he talks back if I speak to him, but he doesn't try to spend time with me alone. He hasn't even started his 'labors.' I guess he's not interested in apologizing after all."

"But he seemed into it when he came to your house over the summer." She nudged my elbow. "You should talk to him. You guys have a tough history. It was always going to be harder with him than with the others, but if you want him, get him."

My head snapped up. "Who says I want him?"

She gave me a knowing look. "You wouldn't be so disappointed right now if you didn't."

"That's not— I didn't— It's not like that," I protested. "I'm already sorting out my feelings for Jaxson, Maverick, and Ezra. I'm not trying to add the massive fucking disaster it would be if Ryder and I got together."

"I don't know who you're trying to fool, but it's not me."

"Sofia!"

Her laughter rang through the room. "Okay, okay. I'll give you a break, but I still think you should talk to him."

"And I think you need to go. Zane will be here to pick you up in a minute."

"I like how you changed the subject."

I pointedly ignored her grin and rescued my jewelry box from her. I held up the teardrop diamond earrings she once said she loved and helped her put them on. "There. Perfect."

"Thanks, Val." She scooped me in a tight hug. "Aren't you going to get dressed?"

I spoke into her hair. "I'm going to be late."

"Why?"

"No date so I might as well wait until the action gets going before making an entrance."

"Okay." She pulled back to look me in the eyes. "But you have to come to the party. We promised that we were finally going to enjoy a year at Evergreen. We're way overdue."

"Fine, I'll come." We heard a knock from downstairs. "That's Zane. See you at the dance."

Sofia practically skipped out the door. I loved that she was so happy. I didn't want to take that away.

My eyes traveled to the phone lying on my nightstand.

Not like Ace is trying to take away mine.

The texts hadn't stopped since yesterday. The floodgates had opened as my unknown harasser taunted me with what they wanted me to do—warning me of the consequences if I refused.

My feet were soundless as I padded across the carpet to my bathroom. Light flooded the space with a single flick and I met my reflection in the mirror. I saw the tears roll down her face. I watched her hand shake as she reached for the scissors.

I saw the moment she realized she was trapped.

MY GOWN TICKLED THE blades of grass as I glided across the quad. Eyes followed me as I went, beating into me like physical blows. I held my head high, eyes fixed on the sports complex and the banner hanging over the beautifully decorated doors.

Cade and Ciara sat at a table before the entrance, checking people in. The line of people shifted to stare at me as I approached.

"—can check your coats and your bags here. Then—" Ciara's eyes popped when she looked up at me. "Valentina?!"

"What the hell did you do to yourself?" Cade threw in.

I marched past all of them without a second glance.

Stepping into the gym was like walking into another world, or maybe another country. Paris had come alive in Evergreen Academy. Soft lighting warmed the space and cast its glow on the mini Eiffel Tower set behind the deejay. Iron tables like you would find outside of a Parisian café were scattered around the dance floor. This was Evergreen, so instead of a buffet table, black-tie waiters swept through the party with trays loaded down with treats. The room was something to behold, and yet, when I walked in, everyone looked at me.

How could I blame them? I had done my best, but a razor would have been better for the hack job Ace demanded I do to my hair. Lock after lock had fallen into the sink, mixing with my tears, as I cut my growing chestnut hair down to the scalp.

"Wow." A voice made me turn my head. A pack of junior boys were posted up near the drinks table. The appetizers were forgotten in their hands as they looked at me with varying degrees of disbe-lief. "Why the fuck did you do that to yourself?" asked Darren. "You look terrible."

Eyes stinging, I fought back against the despair that roared up. "Bald head or no head," I shot back, "I look ten times better than your toady ass."

I flipped him off as his buddies howled. Darren's face crumpled into a sneer. "What the fuck did you just—"

He broke off. Behind him, his friends' laughter dried up as the scowl melted off his face.

"What were you going to say, Rosewood?"

I spun around. Inches from my nose was a hard chest. Maverick towered over me, but his eyes were for them.

"I'm waiting, Rosewood. You have something to say to Valenti-na. I want to hear it."

"I-I was going to tell her... that I like her new look."

"That's what I thought." He jerked his head and that was all it took to hear the sound of their retreat.

My eyes were stinging worse than ever. The lump growing in my throat threatened to choke me as I spoke. "You didn't have to do that," I whispered.

"Of course I did." He placed his finger under my chin and tilted my head up until I saw the soft smile on his lips. "I like the new look too."

"No, you don't." I shook him off. "It's awful and I know it. You don't have to make me feel better."

"I'm not. Why wouldn't I like it?" He took my chin once more. "I did the bald thing too, but on you, it's actually cute." A tear trav-eled down my cheek that he gently wiped away. "Everything about you is beautiful, Valentina."

His words slipped in and pushed back against the rage and vi-olation trying to overtake me. "Maverick," I whispered. It was all I could manage, but I didn't feel I needed to say more.

"Come." Maverick's hand left my cheek to curl around my fin-gers. "Dance with me."

I quickly rubbed at my eyes. "I thought I was the only one al-lowed to see you dance."

"I'm making an exception just this once."

Maverick led me through the stares and whispers to the middle of the dance floor. Ace could have been among the crowd, basking in their victory over me, but as Maverick placed his hands on my waist and pulled me close, I forgot all about them.

"You really do look amazing."

"Thank you." I rested my head against his chest, breathing him in.

Sofia had gone with fun and flirty, but the gown I chose was different in every way. Waves of tulle fell to the floor in a shim-mering green waterfall. A matching drawstring purse hung from my wrist, bumping me as we swayed. My front was covered by a jew-eled top while my back was exposed to the warmth of Maverick's hand. He trailed his thumb along my spine, rubbing slow circles that made me shiver.

"Are you going to the party after this?"

"Sofia wants me to go, but I can't say I'm eager to go back there again. I can't tell her that though."

"Then tell her you'll be with me. I don't want to go there either. So why don't you come back to my... room with me?" Nerves crept into his voice. "There's something I want to show you."

"Maverick Beaumont." I looked up at him so he could get the full force of my grin. "Is that a euphemism?"

His eyes popped. "What? No! I mean— Not that I don't want to. If you want to— But that wasn't what I— I do want—"

"You do?" I slid my hands over his chest and draped them around his shoulders. "What do you want to do?"

He lowered his head, resting it against my forehead as he closed his eyes. "Fuck, Valentina. I want to take you back and show you something... and if more happens, I want that too."

"Maybe more will happen, if I like this something."

"Oh, you'll like it. Trust me." Said in that deep, husky voice, the words were a straight shot to my core. My pulse quickened as Maverick drew me in.

"Maybe we should go see it now."

His hand tightened on my waist. "I can't." He sounded like the words hurt him to say. "There are three more Knights dying to dance with the queen."

"Three?" *He can't mean Ryder?*

"Yes. All I ask is that I get to be with you after the dance."

"I can make that happen." I rose on the tips of my toes, seeking his lips.

Buzz. Buzz.

I felt the vibrations against my body as Maverick kissed me. It pulled me out of the moment as every message did now, filling me with dread at what the next text would say.

We broke apart moments before I felt a tap on my shoulder.

"Valentina?" My friend's voice turned me away from Maverick. Sofia looked stricken as she stared at my fuzzy brown head. "Can I talk to you?"

Maverick's hands disappeared. "I'll leave you two alone."

Sofia snagged my arm the minute he left. She pulled me off to a shadowed corner behind the drinks table.

"Val, what happened? Why did you cut your hair?"

"I just... wanted a change." I tried to hold her gaze, but looked away.

"Bullshit."

"Sof—"

"Don't 'Sof' me." Sofia folded her arms, staring me down. "I told you that you can't fool me. You've been excited about growing your hair back to the length it was. The first time you cut it was because you were going through some tough shit, and on top of that, you've been acting weird all day. I know something is up. What is it?"

The truth sprung to my lips. I wanted to tell her badly, but even without Ace's warning hanging over my head; she could never know about Scarlett. That was our secret.

"There's nothing, Sofia. You don't have to worry."

"I don't believe you." Her expression softened. "Val, it's me. Tell me what's going on."

Her concern tore at me. She was going to make me cry again after Maverick had so perfectly lifted my spirits. "I don't... know where to start."

She took my hand. "We'll start with stealing a tray, or three, off the waiters and going up to the roof to talk. Whatever it is, we'll figure it out."

I loved her so much I did cry. Tears collected on my lids as I smiled. Ace may have taken my hair, but they could never take away a friend as great as her. "I would like that, but not tonight, okay?" I swiped my hand across my eyes. "I want to have fun tonight—with you, the twins, the boys... Maverick. We earned tonight, remember."

She smiled back. "Yes, we did."

We stepped out of our corner to find two people waiting for us. Zane held out his hand for his girlfriend and Sofia took it immediately. He swept her off as Ezra stepped up to me.

"Is everything okay? Looks like you and Richards were having an intense talk."

"Everything is fine."

"Great, then I can steal you away." He held out his arm which I linked with mine. "Are you hungry? It's quiet on the other side of the gym so we can eat."

"That would be nice."

We weaved through the bodies toward the scent of heavenly food. Out of the corner of my eye, I peeked at Ezra.

"Aren't you going to ask about my hair?"

He shook his head. "No, but I do have a question."

"What?"

"Do you keep the rest of you as hairless? Because I could be into that."

Heat flooded my cheeks. I thought I was getting used to the real Ezra and his love of raunchy jokes, but every day he managed to think of something to make me blush harder. "Ezra!" I hissed. "Will you behave yourself?"

"Around you? Never."

I rolled my eyes. "You're too much."

Together we walked up to a free table, and proving that there were many sides to Ezra Lennox, he pulled out my chair and pushed it in for me to sit. He took his seat and pulled it closer to me.

"The waiters should—"

"Good evening, monsieur et mademoiselle." The man appeared as if summoned. "For your pleasure, we have a lovely onion soup, arugula salad, and the main course, beef bourguignon."

"Delicious," I replied. "Thank you very much."

The man bowed and then left. Ezra's hand found mine under the table.

"You know..."

I held my breath, bracing myself for the questions about my hair.

"...I have one more labor left."

"Oh." I blinked. "But you've already given me what I wanted. I feel like I know you so much more now. Maybe too much."

He cracked a smile. "I hope you're not disappointed."

I wove my fingers through his. "Not even a little."

"I'm glad, but there's still one more thing I want to do to show you that I'm worth it."

"Worth what?"

"You."

Ezra's dark eyes used to be unreadable to me—not anymore. The depths of his emotions shone so clearly, I had to look away or be lost. I leaned forward to rest my head on his shoulder.

"I'm looking forward to it."

We sat there in silence, his cheek pressed against my head until the waiter returned. I roused myself to eat. I could have stayed like that with him for the rest of the night.

"Ezra," I began after finishing my salad. "I was thinking about getting a pass for next weekend. I thought you could get one too."

He froze with the fork hovering over his plate. He shot me a wide-eyed look that confused me. "You mean you want to... go away with me like you did with Jaxson?"

My jaw dropped. "Like I did with Jaxson?"

The fork clattered onto the table. "If you're ready to have sex with me—"

"Ezra, oh my—" If I thought my cheeks were on fire before. "How did you know that's why Jaxson and I went away?"

He cocked his head. "From Jaxson, of course. Did you think he was going to keep it a secret?"

Groaning, I clapped my hand over my face. "What did he *say*?"

"Don't worry, he didn't give us the dirty details." I could hear the amusement in his tone. "He only wanted to make sure we knew we were never going to measure up after that weekend."

"I'm going to kill that guy," I grumbled.

"So why do you want us to get passes?"

I let out a breath, growing serious. "I thought we— I could go speak to your mom. You don't have to come with me, but either way, I'm going to tell her the truth about the football game."

Ezra's grin melted off his face. "Okay. Yeah. Then I will come. It will make more sense to her when I tell her what I did too."

I nodded. "If we are ever going to go away together, then we should have everything out in the open. Start fresh."

Ezra bent closer until I could feel the heat from his body. "We will *go away* together." He loaded that sentence with twice the suggestion. "And when we do, I promise I'll measure up."

Whatever could be said to that, I didn't know.

"I want you, Valentina. I know I don't deserve you, and that I may never have all of you, but you can have all of me."

I rested my head on his shoulder again, heart filling with so many emotions I thought it would burst. "I have a feeling you'll have more of me than you think."

Ezra pulled back. I looked up only for him to capture my lips in a sweet, chaste kiss.

We broke apart, grinning like fools, and finished our food. After, Ezra led me to the dance floor and spun me to a slow song. He kept a respectable distance between us the whole time, but there was nothing respectable about his mouth.

"Do you want to go up to the roof and take advantage of me?"

"Ezra!" I cried, fighting a giggle.

"Just for a little bit." His grin was wicked. "No one will even know we're gone."

I glanced around. *Girl, why are you still here?*

"Okay, just for a little—"

Ezra grabbed my hand and ran off before I could get the words out.

Laughing, we slipped out of the gym and hurried to the back of the building. We burst out onto the roof and I threw him on the couch. I straddled him as we went at each other like starving animals.

Being with Ezra felt wild and dangerous and thrilling all at once—like jumping out of a plane with no parachute. Our lips clashed in a frenzied battle. Moans filled the night sky.

I always wondered how Ezra would kiss me when he didn't have watching eyes keeping him gentlemanly, and now I knew. Kiss was too small a word for what he was doing to me.

Our hands roamed over each other's bodies with abandon and it wasn't enough. I scrabbled at his collar and pulled, ripping open his shirt and exposing his chest to my seeking fingers. But my fingers weren't the only ones seeking.

We were surrounded by a sea of tulle. Ezra slipped his hand under the fabric and found my thigh. The night was cold, but his hands were warm on my body as he moved closer and closer.

I broke our kiss, chest heaving. "Do it."

He didn't wait for another invitation. Ezra's finger slipped inside the fabric of my underwear and found what it was looking for.

I gasped, arching my back as he probed my core. My cries got louder as he picked up speed, pushing me closer to the edge. Ezra cried out too, but my nails were digging so fiercely into his shoulder that might have had something to do with it.

In a breath, fireworks were exploding in the sky, or at least, that's what it seemed like as I collapsed against him.

"Wow," I breathed. We were both panting like we had run miles. "I have to take advantage of you more often."

He chuckled. "That's what I keep saying."

It took a few minutes—and a couple more kisses—to straighten up and go back downstairs. Ezra caught my arm before I could round the corner for the front of the building.

"I have to go back to my dorm and change my shirt. I'll find you later." He gave me one more searing kiss before running off.

I tried to keep the smile off my face as I walked back into the dance. I didn't give a shit about the stares anymore. Ace thought this would get to me—ruin my night. But I had been through so much worse within these very gates.

My eyes swept the room, looking out over my dancing classmates and the professors who watched over them.

If you're here, get a good look. You haven't beaten me.

"Valentina." The call was followed by a hand on my elbow. "Hey, I've been looking for you." Kai turned me to face him. "Where were you?"

Memories flooded my mind. "I was... getting some fresh air. What's up?"

"What do you think?" He jerked his head toward the dance floor. "Let's see who the best dancer really is. America versus South Africa. Right now."

My brows shot up my forehead. "Are you challenging me? You don't want none of this, Thomas."

"Oh, but I do, Moon. I really do."

"Just don't cry when I beat you."

We took off for the dance floor, and I saw right away, Kai Thomas could *not* dance. He was the most uncoordinated, jerky, wild dancer I had ever seen and it was only made better for the fact that he did not give a shit. I was in tears watching him, messing up my own moves every time he had me in stitches.

"Dude, South Africa has lost this round and all rounds until the end of time," I shouted over the music.

"What are you talking about?" Kai stuck out his ass and gave it a wiggle. "You don't think this will win me homecoming king?"

I doubled over howling. "S-stop! I can't breathe!"

"Show me how it's done, then." Suddenly, hands were gripping me. My laughter disappeared as Kai pulled me into his arms. "Teach me how to dance."

I looked around. The speakers were pumping a loud steady stream of hip-hop and pop music, and everyone was dancing as wild and bad as Kai. "But we can't slow dance to this song."

"Forget the song." Kai's arm snaked around my waist. "Forget everyone else."

Kai rocked me back and forth, stepping with more grace than I expected. "You're good at this. Where did you learn?"

I felt his shrug. "A couple of rich boys dragged to their parents' banquets. I picked up a few things."

"Then you don't need me," I replied even as I put my arms around his shoulders.

"No." His voice was soft in my ear. "But you clearly need me. That's the second time you've stepped on my foot."

"Oops, sorry." I tried to pull back to give us some distance, but Kai held me firm.

"It's okay. Just let me lead."

I lifted my head, gazing over Kai's shoulder. Our eyes met immediately.

Jaxson's expression was unreadable as he watched me dance with Kai. I tensed.

His expression is never unreadable. I can always tell what he's thinking with one look, and that I can't now...

"Val, you alright?"

"I'm—"

"Excuse me? Can I cut in?"

My breath caught at the sound of his voice. I pulled away from Kai and there he was. Ryder stood before me as effortlessly gorgeous as he always was. His tux was a black as deep as his raven locks, which he swept out of his eyes with a careless flick before reaching for my hand.

"You... want to dance with me?"

He smiled—that beautiful, rare smile that made bubbles erupt and burst in my stomach. "Who else would I be talking to? I'm not dancing with him."

Despite myself, a laugh escaped my lips. Ryder was still Ryder underneath the handsome exterior. I looked at Kai. "Do you mind?"

"No, it's cool." He dropped his hands. "Go ahead."

Ryder's arms were around me before he finished. As if on cue, the song changed. The heady thumping beat was replaced by a slow song I had never heard before but it captured me with its tune. We fell into the rhythm so easily; it felt like we had been dancing together for years.

"Ryder?" I raised my head to look into his eyes.

"Yes?"

"This is weird."

He barked a laugh. "If you don't want to dance with me—"

"No, it's not that," I said quickly. My grip on his forearms was tight. "I do, but this is strange after the way things have been between us lately. You've been distant, and considering the way you were before, that is saying something."

The corner of his mouth quirked up into a half smile. "You always say exactly what you're thinking, don't you?"

I lifted my chin. "I think that's best. Seriously, Ryder. You said you wanted to show me you were sorry like the other guys, but it's been weeks and we barely talk. Did you change your mind?"

"Of course not. I owe you more apologies than I can give. I've thought about nothing but what I want to do to show you how I feel."

His words made the bubbles go crazy. My stomach fluttered with a rush of feelings I couldn't place.

"So what now?"

"What I want to do for you can wait until the guys have done theirs. I think you'd rather spend more time with them anyway."

Ryder's expression remained neutral as he delivered that. I picked up the meaning behind his words clearly, but it was impossible to guess how he felt about them.

"I want to spend time with all of you, Ryder. Things are different. The five of us; we're bound in ways people will never understand. Not to mention you and me." I stopped dancing and Ryder ground to a halt. It was hard, but I held his gaze as I said, "You know me. You know every deep secret and—"

I placed my hand on his chest. Beneath my palm, his heart raced, beating against me to tell the tale of just how affected he was.

"—I know yours," I whispered. "We can't go back to the way it was so let's move forward. Tell me what you want to do, and we'll do it."

Ryder didn't reply at first. He stared back at me, his gaze unwavering as those silver eyes pulled me in. I couldn't look away, so I noticed the second something flashed in his eyes. For the barest moment, Ryder Shea's mask broke and I felt something that had been stirring deep inside since the night of the roof, coming to life every time our eyes met when no one was looking.

I felt connected to him.

Ryder placed his hand over the one on his chest. "Valentina..."

Buzz. Buzz.

The vibrations jarred me out of the moment as realization smacked me over the head.

Oh no. I never checked my phone after the first message. What if it's—

The music slowed to a reverberating stop. Ryder dropped his hand as someone came on the mic.

"Hello, junior class," Ezra announced. "Are you ready to find out our homecoming king and queen?"

Cheers went up around me but I didn't turn around. My hands fumbled on the drawstrings of my purse, pulling it open to reach inside.

Ace: Bald as an egg and the Knights are still all over you. Let's see if I can get more creative this time.

Ace: Ignoring me? That's okay because I've thought of the perfect thing. This should let them see how much of a worthless slut you really are.

The sides of my phone dug painfully into my palm as I read what they wanted me to do. *Why? Why are you doing this to me?*

I typed the words before I could stop myself.

Ace: Why shouldn't I?

"The Evergreen homecoming king is... Kai Thomas!"

The crowd roared as I shot off my message.

Me: I won't do it!

Ace: You will or I send the video to the police.

Me: What do you want from me?! What's the point of this?!

Ace: I didn't start this game. But I'll finish it.

"—and our homecoming queen." Ezra's voice broke through. "Valentina Moon!"

Ace: Do it.

My hands fell to my sides. Slowly, I turned to face the stage. Ezra and Kai looked back at me, beckoning me up with their smiles as around me my class burst into applause.

One, two, three steps I took until a path was made for me to go the rest of the way. Faces on all sides watching me, and I knew for certain in that moment that Ace was one of them.

I placed my foot on the bottom step. Ezra carried my crown on a pillow. It rested on his palm as he reached out for my hand. I took it, clutching it too tightly if the concerned look he gave me was a clue.

I looked away and my eyes fell on them. Maverick, Jaxson, and Ryder stood at the end of the stage, and Maverick's smile reminded me of what he said that night.

"There are three more Knights dying to dance with the queen."

I wondered if they had anything to do with this. Four Knights crowning me their queen. It was so sweet. If only Ace wouldn't see it ruined.

Ezra pressed his lips to my ear as he put the crown on my head. "Congratulations, Valentina. You deserve it. How about we celebrate after? On the roof."

Equal parts sadness and desire flooded me in a stomach-churning mix. "I'd like that," I whispered.

He pulled back and smiled—a smile that was just for me.

"Okay, everyone." Ezra turned his charm on the crowd. "Let's give it up for our king and queen."

Beaming, Kai grabbed my hand and held ours up. "I'm never going to let Zane live this down. I told him everyone likes me more."

I shook my head. Kai really was sweet and funny. He spun me around to face him, pulling me in as he did.

"We're supposed to dance for our subjects, right." Kai gave me a lopsided grin. "It's a good thing we practiced."

"Yes," I said softly. "Good thing."

"The king and queen will have their dance," Ezra echoed. "Then we'll announce the rest of the royal..."

His words faded as I gazed at Kai. My arms went around his shoulders as his moved to my waist. The nape of his neck was soft beneath my hand. His brown curls brushed my fingertips as I curled my hand around his neck.

I didn't stop to think. I leaned in and captured Kai's lips in a butterfly kiss.

Gasps filled the room, but none as loud as the whoops and cat-calls. They sounded all around us, and still I heard Ezra cut himself off with a sharp intake of breath.

Kai didn't respond at first, then his grip on me tightened. He drew me closer and deepened the kiss.

Screech!

Microphone feedback assaulted my ears. I tore my lips away to see the back of Ezra as he stomped off the stage.

I broke out of Kai's arms. "Ezra, wait!"

He didn't look back. Ezra shoved through the other Knights and the looks on their faces stopped me cold. One by one, they turned and followed him until only Ryder was left. When he turned away, the cold perfect mask had returned to his face as though it had never left.

Chapter Eight

"Val? Val, are you in here?"

I glanced up from my phone. Ace's message shown stark on my screen.

Ace: Ignoring me? That's okay because I've thought of the perfect thing. This should let them see how much of a worthless slut you really are. I want you to kiss your stupid lovesick friend, Kai Thomas, and make sure the Knights see.

"Val, come on." Sofia knocked on the bathroom stall. "I know you're in there. Come out."

"I'm coming."

Sofia pulled me into a strangling hug the second I stepped out. "Val, you were crying."

The ache behind my eyes and my stuffed nose told of the tale. I ran to the bathroom after the Knights walked out on me. I cried to the sound of Kai pounding on the door asking if I was okay.

"Yes."

She pulled back and held me at arm's length. "What happened up there? I thought you weren't interested in Kai."

"I'm not." My tears began anew. "I only see him as a friend. A good friend. Now I've messed everything up with him and... and..."

"The Knights." Sofia guided me over to the chaise and made me sit down. She pulled my head down onto her shoulder. "I don't understand, Val. Why did you kiss him if you feel that way?"

My phone was still in my hand. I thought it might crack into parts for how hard I gripped it. "It was... just a mistake."

"You don't make mistakes like that." I blinked at the steel in her voice. "You'd never do anything to hurt your friend. Tell me what's going on, Val. The truth."

"Sofia, there's nothing—"

"Stop. No more of that. Tell me."

I wanted to keep fighting her. If I hadn't been so worn out with the vision of the Knights turning their backs on me playing in my mind, I might have kept saying no.

"I'm being blackmailed," I replied through numb lips. My tears had dried up. I felt nothing but empty.

"Blackmailed? By who?"

"I don't know who it is, but they forced me to cut my hair and kiss Kai. They want to break me."

"But why?" Sofia twisted so she could meet my eyes. Hers were round and frightened. "Who would do that? What are they threatening you with?"

My fuzzy mind thought quickly. I couldn't tell her about Scarlett. That was a secret that would remain between me and the Knights... and Ace.

"They found out about Adam," I lied. "They know he's my son and who his father is."

She sucked in a breath as I tamped down on my guilt. "How could they have found out?"

"I wish I knew." I dropped my gaze. "I don't know who or how, but I can't let them tell anyone what they know. They have me, Sofia, and they know it."

Sofia grabbed my chin and made me look at her. "We have to find out who this piece of shit is. I can't believe anyone would be so soulless that they would blackmail you over your son. We'll find them and stop them."

I grabbed her and hugged her tight. "I'm trying," I said into her hair. "I called the hacker again to trace the number. The only thing I'm sure of is that they were at the dance tonight. They saw me with the boys."

"That narrows them down. We'll get them, Val, but first, you have to find the guys."

"Ezra was so mad—"

"Because he doesn't know the truth. Tell them."

"I can't." I released her and sat back. "Ace told me not to tell anyone about them. If the boys know, they'll go after them. If Ace finds out then they'll tell the whole world my secret."

Sofia didn't reply. An odd expression came over her face as I spoke. "What did you just say?" she whispered.

"Ace warned me about—"

Sofia's hand flashed out. I yelped as she seized my hand hard enough to hurt. "That's the name they've been using? They've been calling themselves Ace?"

There was an intensity in her voice that freaked me out. "Yes, why?"

"Ace, Val. Ace as in... Ace of Spades."

"THEY MIGHT BE THERE. I saw Ryder go into the woods when Zane left."

Twigs snapped beneath our heels as we made our way through the trees. It might have been the most private spot for secret parties, but I hated the way the darkness pressed in on me—silent and absolute. The cliffs were the last place on earth I wanted to be.

"Sofia." I glanced across at her. Shadows covered her face, but I didn't need to see her to guess her expression. "Are you sure?"

"No." Her words traveled through the eerie darkness. "No one is sure. That's on purpose. But that is what most people think. There is an 'A' on the back of the card. An 'A' was on the back of your joker card, Val. No one knows for sure but many people think that A is for Ace."

"Ace of Spades."

"Exactly. That letter must be on the back for a reason. It could be a signature."

"You think this Ace person is behind the marks?"

"That's what a lot of people think, but aren't stupid enough to say out loud."

I fell silent. *I've never thought too hard about what the letter meant, but one thing is certain, I knew exactly who marked me, and they aren't texting me now.*

"It never ends, does it?" I felt her eyes on me. "The secrets, the lies, the fear, the hold the Spades have over this school. It's never going to stop."

No more words passed between us as we headed for the light breaking through the trees. The party was in full swing when we stepped out into the clearing. The fire raged, and all around it, smartly dressed rich kids and geniuses danced, drank, and let loose.

Zane burst from the clutches of the party, making his way over to us.

"This is going to stop, Val." I glanced at my best friend. "We're going to end this. I promise."

She gave my hand one last squeeze before Zane claimed her.

I held back. My eyes passed over the sea of faces looking for four in particular.

Please be here. I have to explain. Please—

Blue eyes locked with mine first. Four chairs were placed only a few feet away from the edge, and my Knights sat in them looking over the party—looking at me.

The party blurred around me as my feet carried me over to them. They sat far enough away that the noise fell to a dull roar when I finally stopped in front of Jaxson.

He smiled at me. "What's up, baby?"

"Jaxson, I—" I looked from him to Maverick, Ezra, and Ryder. "I want to explain what happened."

"No need." The smile remained on Jaxson's lips. "You can kiss whoever you want. We're not exclusive."

"Of course, Moon." My head swung to Ezra. The charming, mannequin-man look that he knew I hated hid his feelings away. "I shouldn't have gotten upset. If you like Thomas, then that's fine."

"Date him." Maverick got to his feet and the others followed suit. "It doesn't change how we feel about you."

Panic filled me as they turned their backs. Despite Maverick's promise, I could feel something had shifted. I had lost them. Ace had won.

That thought propelled me forward. "No, wait!" I grabbed Maverick's arm. "Please, just let me explain. I don't like him. Not like that. It's— It's you." The words tumbled from my mouth and there was no way to stop them. All of the feelings that had been torturing me for the last few weeks welled up and tipped over.

"I want you," I repeated as they finally turned to me. I looked into Maverick's eyes. "I want you."

My gaze drifted to Ezra. "I want you."

Then Jaxson, my sweet goofball. "I want you."

"And I w-want—" The firelight danced in his silver eyes as ours met. Ryder looked at me steadily and the words stuck in my throat. I couldn't get them out, but yet I could not stop. "It's been killing me feeling that I have to choose, but... knowing that I never could. There's no room in my heart for Kai, because it's taken up by you."

Ezra moved first. I didn't have time to react before he took my face in his hands and kissed me. My pain and uncertainty burned away in the heat of our clashing lips.

"Then why?" he asked when we broke apart. "Why did you kiss him?"

"I didn't want to." I took a shuddering breath. "I'm being blackmailed by someone who calls themselves Ace."

"The fuck?" Jaxson pushed Ezra aside. "Blackmailed? For how long? Why didn't you say something?"

"Because they were there that day. They have a video of..." My voice trailed off as I looked over their shoulders. Darkness swallowed the rim of the cliff, but I knew what awaited me if I stepped to the edge. I knew who lay at the bottom.

Ryder followed my line of sight. I saw the moment when it hit him. He snapped his head around, nostrils flaring. "We need to go. Now."

"But—" Ryder pushed through the boys, grabbed my hand, and dragged me off. The boys fell in line beside us. "Where are we going?"

"My room."

Ryder kept a tight hold of my hand as we stomped through the woods. No one said anything as we went, but I did not question why. We knew now that someone was always listening and watching.

The junior dorm was ghostly quiet when we stepped inside and made our way to Ryder's room. He set me down on his bed before the questioning began.

"Tell us everything."

Ryder stood, but Jaxson and Maverick sat down on either side of me, relaxing me with their presence. Ezra claimed the desk chair and scooted close enough to take my hand. My heart pounded as he laced our fingers together. I was with my Knights. Everything would be okay.

I let out a steadying breath. "It all started the first week of school. I've been getting texts from a person who calls themselves Ace."

Ryder stepped closer. "You said they have a video."

"They do. Of the moment Scarlett went over the cliff."

"Did you actually see it?" Jaxson asked. "How do you know they are for real?"

"They sent it to me."

A tense silence followed my statement.

"They said they would send the video to the police if I didn't do what they wanted."

"This is what you were talking about before," said Maverick. "That's why you wanted to know if you could trace a number."

"Yes." I sighed. "Not that it worked. My hacker tried but the number led to a burner phone. She couldn't help me."

A finger caressed my cheek and I turned to see the concern etched into Jaxson's face. "Why didn't you tell us sooner?"

"They told me not to say anything about them." I leaned into his touch. "I'm sorry. Tonight went too far and I couldn't let you think that something was going on with me and Kai." I shook my head. "I'll have to talk to him too. Find a way to explain what happened."

"Worry about him later." Jaxson passed a hand over my fuzzy head. "Did that shit stain make you cut your hair too?"

I nodded.

His face tightened. "Fucking hell. Why?"

"I think... because of you."

He blinked. "Me?"

"Yes." I reached into my bag and pulled out my phone. I tried to hand it to Jaxson, but Ryder bent down and intercepted it. He was quiet as he read Ace's texts, although his face said so much more. The cool granite mask was nowhere to be found.

"She's right," he announced. "They mention how much Jaxson likes playing with her hair before telling her to cut it off. They get mad that it wasn't enough to turn us away. Then they tell her to kiss Thomas in front of us."

Cursing, Jaxson snatched the phone from his hands. "This is about us?! Why? Who is this fuck? Why would they care if we're with Valentina?"

The words were out of my mouth before I could stop them. "Scarlett would care."

Four pairs of eyes flew to me.

"Scarlett's dead," said Ezra, voice hard.

"I know she's dead. There's no way she survived that fall. But think of who she was. She was a Spade and you were the Knights that were going to make her problem go away: me. Instead, you chose me." I gestured at my phone. "I've been thinking about this since Sofia told me the significance of that name. If they're a Spade too, then they know their chosen Knights were connected to the death of one of them and took it on themselves to lift the mark."

Ryder tossed his head. "This person doesn't say anything about Knights, Spades, or marks, Val."

"Yes, but why are they calling themselves Ace like the letter on the back of the marks?"

"Maybe they're calling themselves Ace to freak you out." This came from Maverick. He had finally spoken up. "That's what it most likely is. You've seen the kind of damage a real Spade can do. They don't have to play games like this when they can get others to do their dirty work. This can't be them."

"We don't know that there is a *them*," Ezra added. "We ended that with Scarlett, but clearly there was someone else in the woods that day. In the wrong place at the right time and they're using this for some creepy crusade."

"They don't want me with you."

"Tough shit." Jaxson placed a kiss on my forehead. "You're stuck with us."

I cracked a smile. "I could be okay with that."

"Seriously, guys." Ezra rose to his feet. "What are we going to do? This person is sick. We can't let them jerk around Valentina, but we can't let that video get out either."

Ryder inclined his head. "If they are trying to get between us and Val, we let them think this worked. We keep our distance."

"What does keep our distance mean?" Jaxson demanded.

"You know what it means. No more hand-holding in the halls. No more visits to her dorm. No more whisking her away to the beach."

My cheeks warmed. The boys really did talk.

"And if that doesn't work?"

"It's only to get them to back off while we—"

"While we find them," Maverick finished. "I'll track down whoever is doing this and stop it for real."

I shivered. Maverick was my sweet, soft-spoken one. Hearing that hard edge to his voice was new for me. It was time for me to say something.

"Guys, I know you want to protect me, but I don't want to see what happens if we push Ace. We're all in trouble if that video gets out."

"That's why we need to find them and get rid of it," Ezra argued. "Val, there's no way we sit by and do nothing."

Ryder's gaze was unwavering as he nodded. "We promised we would protect you. That's what we're going to do."

"But, guys, I can handle my—"

Jaxson tugged my arm and pulled me to his chest. I was enfolded into his sweet scent in a blink. "You're not going to win this one, mama, so I'd give up now. We're Knights. We're your Knights. This is what we do."

I should have argued more, but Jaxson felt so warm memories of us comfortable and giggling beneath my sheets flooded my mind. If moments like this were truly going to be rare from now on, I didn't want to waste time fighting about it.

I burrowed into his side as we went back and forth, figuring out a plan. Two hours later, I was hoarse and feeling like the equivalent of a wrung-out dishrag, but still, we knew what we would do.

"So, Maverick, you'll hook up with Valentina's hacker and find out everything you can about this guy," Ryder stated. "Ezra, ask around. Whoever it is was there at the promenade and the dance. We know it's a junior or one of the junior professors."

"If this has to do with the Spades," I said, "then we need to look closer at the professors. Five came with us to chaperone."

"That won't be easy. They have no reason to tell us anything and getting to their files is impossible. Maverick tried everything to get into the system to find out more about Scarlett."

"There has to be a way."

"If there is, we'll find it. In the meantime"—Ryder fixed Jaxson with a look—"we keep our distance in public."

"Don't look at me," Jaxson scoffed. "I won't do anything to risk Val, but this shit's not forcing us into a life of celibacy either."

I tilted back and flicked his forehead. "Will you stop thinking about sex for a minute?"

He grinned. "Not likely. I've thought about sex with you *every* minute since I met you."

Rolling my eyes, I slipped out of his arms and stood. "We know what we have to do. We'll find them and end this." I bent to gather my stuff.

"Where are you going?" asked Ezra.

"We don't want anyone to see me here. I should head out before people come back from the party."

"Wait." A voice stopped me halfway to the door. "Val, don't you remember...?"

"Oh." I turned back to Maverick. A flush moved up my neck at the memory of what we planned at the dance. "Of course. I... still want to see it."

Jaxson looked between me and him. "See what?"

Maverick came over and took my hand without answering. "Night, guys."

Together, we left 208 and padded across to 204. Maverick didn't bother to shield the keypad as he typed in his code. I hoped he couldn't hear my erratic heartbeat. It sounded so loud in my ears I was sure it would wake the whole hall.

A soft chime and then Maverick was pushing into his bedroom. I stepped inside as he flicked on the lights, taking it all in. Maverick's bedroom was the same layout as Ryder's but that is where the similarities stopped. His room was a mess of parts, gadgets, tools, and electronics taking up every surface. It wasn't that it was messy; it was just that there was so much he was creating and so little space.

"Sorry about all of this." He stepped into the middle of his room. He stood there looking around with the cutest expression on his face. "I tried to clean up before the dance."

I smiled. "You knew I was coming?"

"I hoped you would come."

"What did you want to show me?" I brought my hand to my collarbone and gently brushed my strap off my shoulder. "I can't wait to see it."

Maverick's eyes darted to my bare flesh. I saw his eyes darken as he licked his lips. "It's uh... over here."

He looked away with obvious reluctance and got on his knees. My seductive smirk disappeared as I watched him crawl to his bed and stick his head beneath the mattress.

Maybe this isn't a sexy surprise. Am I about to be treated to some kind of deep secret?

"Hey, guys."

Guys?

I knelt down as Maverick pulled out the basket. Gasping, I clapped my hand over my mouth. "Maverick, oh my gosh." Nestled within the folds of a blanket, two balls of black and white fuzz blinked at me in the light. "They're so cute."

Maverick picked one of the kittens up and placed them in my waiting hands. "I found him and his sister near the gates last week. I've been checking on them, and when their mother stopped coming, I brought them in here." He ducked his head. "I thought you'd like to see them."

"I do." I nuzzled the little furry head. The kitten mewled—a soft, weak sound that was accompanied by a rumbling purr. "It's been so long since I've been around pets. Mom doesn't want something else to look after and they're not allowed here." I grinned at him. "Speaking of which, is this another thing the Knights are allowed to get away with?"

He laughed. "No. I'm pretty sure I'd get in trouble too if anyone found these guys." Maverick picked up the other kitten and held her against his chest. She was so tiny she fit perfectly in the palm of his hand. She must have found it comfortable too because she closed her eyes and went back to sleep. "I'm going to get a pass and bring them home this weekend."

"Are your parents cool with that?"

"Mom and Dad are used to me bringing home strays. We're up to five dogs, three cats, a turtle, and a cockatiel now."

"I've got to come by your place and meet all these pets."

"You can come with me this weekend." Maverick moved closer until he was pressing against my side. "My parents will be home, but I'd like you to get to know them."

"I'd like that too," I confessed as I rubbed the purrball against my cheek. "But I'm going to Ezra's this weekend to talk to his mom."

"Next weekend then." Maverick lowered his head and kissed my bare shoulder. The act made goose bumps erupt on my body. "It's going to be next to impossible to hold myself back around you. At least if we're off campus, we can still be together."

"I have a feeling I'm going to be requesting a lot of weekend passes from now on," I whispered. "Mom's going to get suspicious."

He shrugged. "Use them to visit her and your brother, but on the way up and down, you can take... detours."

"Sexy and wicked smart. I always said you were dangerous, Maverick Beaumont."

Maverick dropped kisses along my neck to my collarbone, laughing softly as he went. "Not me. I'm the harmless computer geek, introverted jock." He pressed his lips to my neck and I leaned back, giving him better access.

"Next weekend," I agreed. "Let's take a detour."

"We will."

Maverick stopped his tantalizing journey up my neck. I looked at him in confusion until he reached for the sleeping kitten. He placed them gently in their basket and pushed it back under the bed. I now had his full attention.

I didn't have time to get nervous before he was putting his arm around my waist and the other beneath my knees. I let out a soft exclamation as he hoisted me bridal style in his arms.

He set me on the comforter and I sank into its downy arms. My breath caught as Maverick shrugged off his jacket. He moved to his buttons and undid them with agonizing slowness, not looking away from me the whole time.

It was me that broke contact when his fingers moved to his belt. I didn't want to miss this. The leather was pulled through the loop and dropped to the floor. His pants soon followed.

My breaths came quicker as my core pulsed with desire. We hadn't started but I was already aching for him.

Maverick held his hand out to me. "Come here. I'll help you with that."

I rose to my knees and turned, giving him my back. My heart hammered in my chest as the sound of my zipper filled the room.

This wasn't Jaxson's passionate eagerness or Ezra's red-hot frenzy. Maverick acted as though he had all the time in the world to make love to me, and he would savor every second.

He pushed the dress down to my knees and I carefully stepped out of it. I knelt on the bed in nothing but my strapless bra, thong, and heels. Maverick brushed a finger on the nape of my neck and slowly traced a path down my spine. He reached my bra hooks but kept going. Moving over the curves of my ass, then my thighs, then my legs, and finally my heels.

I listened to the *thud, thud* as they fell to the floor. I reached behind me and grasped his hands. There were only two more things for him to take off, and I wanted them off now. His teasing was driving me crazy.

I placed his hands over my breasts. His breathing grew ragged and I knew I was having the same effect on him. I tilted my head back and his lips found mine instantly. As he kissed me, his expert hands made short work of my bra. We broke apart panting as he hooked his fingers through my panties.

"Fuck," he breathed. "You are so incredible."

I giggled. "Thank you. Just wait until you see what's next." I leaned forward and thrust my ass in the air. Maverick slipped my thong off with no more invitation.

Naked, I flipped over and lay before him. His eyes swept over my body the way a starving man looked at a buffet, and when those boxers finally came off, mine did the same.

His muscles rippled as he climbed onto the bed and stalked toward me. I was awarded a kiss on the lips before he began moving down. He passed through the valley of my breasts, over my belly button, and then settled between my legs.

A moan ripped from my throat. I said this guy was dangerous. A geeky, introverted jock sure, but one that knew what he was doing. Again, he took his time, not stopping until he brought me to the edge and I crashed with a hoarse cry.

I watched him through a haze as he reached into the nightstand and pulled out the condom. "Are you ready?"

I nodded, not altogether sure if I was capable of speaking. He positioned himself between my legs and settled his body over me. His movements drove me out of my mind all on their own, but that on top of the hands traveling over every inch of me, the lips kissing my jaw, and the sweet nothings pouring from him; sunbursts were exploding in my mind before I knew it.

"W-wow." My chest heaved as I tried to catch my breath. I threw my arms around his neck. "Let's do that again."

THE GENTLE TICKING of the clock was the only sound in the room as Maverick and I lay beneath his sheet. It told me that it was three a.m. Reminded me that I had to sneak out before anyone found out I was here, but its reminder wasn't enough to pull me from his arms.

There was nothing about Maverick that was typical. He couldn't be predicted. I said I had him all figured out, but the truth was he was constantly surprising me. What did I think sex with the rich boy jock would be but wild? Instead, Maverick treated me like precious porcelain. His touch was gentle. His every act meant to make me feel safe as well as pleasure.

His fingers drew slow circles on my hip. It was the power of his touch that I couldn't fall asleep for that finger.

"Val?"

"Yes?" My head was tucked beneath his chin. His words vibrated in his chest as he spoke.

"I hope I measured up."

A laugh burst out of me before I could stop it. "Maverick, haven't you learned to ignore Jaxson by now? You have nothing to measure up to. My time with him and my time with you are special in their own ways. And this time was—what was the word you used—incredible."

"Oh yeah," he said gruffly, desire lacing his voice. "It was."

I shivered just thinking about our night together. "Today started so awful and now we're here. Maybe I should thank Ace for finally forcing me to tell you guys how I feel."

"You want to date all of us."

"I do." I lifted my head to look him in the eyes. "But what about you? Are you okay with this?"

I could see his smile through the dark. "I was always okay with it. I told you, Valentina. I don't deserve you. I never did. But if being with you means sharing with my best friends, at least I know they'll spend every day proving their worth like I will."

"You won't believe me if I tell you that you don't have to prove yourself anymore, will you?"

"Nope."

I chuckled. "Well, I guess you do have one more labor left."

"I have two more."

"No, we can count the kittens as number two."

"Oh." I could see his smile disappear. "I don't think we should. I used them to get you over here. 'I want to show you something' was totally a euphemism."

"Maverick," I cried, swatting his shoulder. We dissolved into laughter. "So this was all a part of your plan. I said sexy and smart was a wicked combination."

"That wasn't the only part of my plan."

"No?" I scooted up and planted a kiss on his cheek. "What else did you have in mind?"

Maverick's hand found my waist. The finger began anew, drawing circles that sent ripples through my body. "I was planning on telling you... that I love you."

The breath escaped my lungs. *Could I have heard him right? He loves me? Maverick Beaumont loves me?*

"Maverick, I—"

He rose and captured my lips in a slow, sweet kiss. "You don't have to say anything now," he whispered when we broke apart. "I just wanted you to know how I feel."

I nodded, then I bent to kiss him again, hoping it told him how I felt.

"So," he began when I lay back down. "You weren't thinking about sleeping tonight, were you?"

His lips had to swallow my giggling.

THE SUN WAS PEEKING over the horizon when I made it back to my dorm the next morning. I had a lazy Saturday ahead of me—video chatting with Adam, watching movies, tidying up my room, and plotting how I would take Ace down.

The boys had their plan, and it was a good one, but it was me they targeted. Me they violated. My friend they forced me to hurt. My relationships they tried to sabotage. I didn't want to be the girl

I was in sophomore year, but I wasn't letting anyone get away with what they had done to me.

Game on, Ace.

Chapter Nine

"Val, can you pass me the goggles?"

"Sure."

Eric pressed them to his head in a salute. "Thanks. So you ready for the trip? My bag has been packed for the last week."

I replied as we headed for our desks. "Everyone is skipping over this Mt. Providence trip while I'm counting in my head how many times I'm going to fall flat on my face in the snow."

"Ooh. I'll put a bet on that."

Laughing, I shoved his shoulder. It was crazy how easily Eric and I had fallen into our old friendship. I would never forget what he did, but it was nice to forgive him, while I focused my attention on Ace.

"What are you guys laughing about?" Ciara asked when we strolled up.

I handed her a pair of goggles as I took my seat. We had ended up lab partners again. We had never been very close, but that also meant her betrayal hadn't stung as badly. It was easier for us to start over.

"The winter trip. It's going to be insane."

She shook her head. "No, finals are going to be insane, and we have to get through those before we go anywhere."

"Gotta ruin the mood, don't cha," Eric grumbled.

"My dad expects me to get top in the class this year," Ciara replied. "I need a miracle to beat Cade."

"You can do it," I spoke up. "You're definitely getting us an A in chemistry."

She laughed. "You helped."

"That's enough talking." The professor leveled a glare in our direction so we had no doubt who he was talking to. "Start your experiments."

Eric turned around in his seat and we did as ordered. We worked quietly until class let out and then Ciara and Eric went one way while I went the other. I hurried to my locker to pick up my things and then headed for the library.

My pace slowed as I got closer until I stopped dead outside the doors.

Let's do this, Val. No point putting it off.

I took a deep breath then pushed into the library. Kai looked up from his laptop when I approached his table. He got right to it the second my butt hit the seat.

"I read over the paper again and I think it's almost done. I just want to rewrite the conclusion."

"Okay." I took out my computer and dropped my bag at my feet. "The presentation is done too. All that's left is to work out what we're going to say."

"We can do that today."

"Good."

"Great."

We fell silent. Outwardly, Kai looked unbothered but inside I was cringing. Things had been so awkward with us since the homecoming dance. I found him the day after and tried to talk, but he shut me down before I got a word out. He said we should pretend it didn't happen and go back to being friends, but things had been weird ever since. I wanted to fix it, but I didn't know what to tell him then any more than I do now. How do I explain being black-mailed?

I worked on putting the finishing touches on our English lit project while sneaking glances at him out of the corner of my eye. Kai tip-tapped away, his eyes glued to the screen. The need to break the silence pressed on me. This was silly. We are friends. We have to fix this.

"Are you excited for the winter trip?"

I winced internally. Of all the things to say, I went with that.

A small wrinkle appeared between his brows. "Um, yeah. It will be nice to get out of Evergreen land for a bit."

"Still want me to teach you how to ski?"

He cracked a smile. "From someone who has never seen snow? Sounds like a great way to spend the trip with my face in the ice."

"I'll be doing the same. Eric's taking bets on how many times I wipe out."

He laughed—a real, full laugh like the way he used to with me. It spurred me on.

"Sofia will be wrapped up with Zane so it will still be you and me. Want to hang out over the trip?"

His smile held. "I thought we were already doing that."

A niggle of happiness broke through and fed my grin. "We are."

"Good."

"Great."

I went back to our presentation feeling better about us than I had for a while. I didn't have many good friends that I could trust. I wanted to hang on to all of them.

An hour later, our English project was done and we were saying goodbye outside the door. My phone buzzed as I headed back to my dorm and I paused beside the grand window. I had come to dread that buzz.

Ace hadn't ordered me to do anything else since the dance, and it was no doubt because Ryder was right. What they wanted was the Knights to turn their backs on me and I knew that from the constant messages they sent lording it over me.

Ace: They turned on you so quickly. I wonder what they'd do if the video gets out.

Ace: I guess not even your skills in bed could keep them around.

Ace: It was only a matter of time before they found out you were nothing but a diseased slut.

I opened my phone to these messages almost every time I took it out of the box. I wanted to shoot back every harsh reply that came to my mind. I wanted them to know I was coming after them hard. Instead, I bore it in silence. They weren't forcing me to do anything else and I could still be with the boys in secret. Provoking them wasn't the smart move right now.

With that thought in my head, I took out my phone and glanced at the screen. My shoulders slumped with relief when I saw it was Jaxson.

Jaxson: Hey, baby. Did you get a pass for this weekend?

Me: No, I couldn't. Evergreen said no passes before finals. He also gave me his steepled-fingered frown over how many I've used this semester. I think he's going to start cracking down.

Jaxson: The guy needs a daily update that we're not prisoners. This sucks, but we'll be together at Mt. Providence.

Me: But we can't. We'll all be on top of each other in the same resort. What if we get caught?

Jaxson: I'll be on top of you in the same resort.

The number of wink emojis he sent me were outrageous.

Jaxson: Some things are worth it, baby. I'm dying over here.

I rolled my eyes even while a smile played on my lips. Jaxson and I had snuck away on a weekend pass only two weeks ago. The week after that I had been with Maverick. It was no wonder Evergreen was raising his eyebrows, but whether he liked it or not, I was loving getting to see my family almost every weekend—not to mention the detours on the way.

Me: We'll see what happens when we get there. I'm sure there will be little hideaways.

Jaxson: We'll find every one.

From there Jaxson's texts morphed into highly detailed descriptions of the things he wanted to do with me in those hideaways. I'll admit, by the time the need for sleep made me put my phone on the nightstand and turn off the lights, I was looking forward to the trip too.

"WE HAVE TO DO EVERYTHING on this list. First is cocoa by the fire. I'm planning on being ridiculously cliché."

"With me?" I picked her bag off the ground and threw it under the bus after mine. "Aren't you going to be cliché-ing it up with Zane?"

"Of course, but we're not going to get to spend Christmas together this year." She lowered her list to give me a sad smile. "We're going to England to spend the holidays with Dad's mom so no winter village with Adam or sneaking your mom's extra strong eggnog."

"You're going to have so much more fun in England than stuck in my little neighborhood."

She pulled me in for a hug. "No, I won't."

I hugged her back just as tight. The truth was I was going to miss her too. I had gotten used to spending all my vacations with my best friend. She had become a part of our traditions. Not only would I not see her, but Jaxson was going to the Caribbean again. Maverick was visiting relatives out of state. Ezra's mom was taking him to New Zealand, and Ryder's plans were known only to him. It would be just me, Olivia, and Adam once again.

"But until then," I said as we pulled back. "We are going to have a great time at the ski resort. Sign me up for the whole list."

"Everyone, your attention, please."

Professor Markham stood before the wrought-iron gates looking very official with her clipboard. Falling in line next to her was Professor Coleman, Professor Felton, and the headmaster himself.

I eyed Evergreen as Sofia and I joined the circle of juniors forming around them. It was odd seeing the headmaster outside of his office. He only emerged if it was time to hand down punishments. Otherwise, he was a stern face on the screen or behind his desk.

"Good evening," Evergreen began. "I know you are all looking forward to your trip so I will make it brief. The resort has been booked out so you will be the only guests, but that does not change my expectations. You are to conduct yourself in a manner benefiting representatives of this elite institution." His gaze swept over each of us individually. "There will be no drinking, no gambling, no roughhousing, no inappropriate dress, and no funny business. Am I understood?"

"Yes, sir," we chorused.

Evergreen's stern expression did not lessen. "We'll see." With those parting words, the headmaster turned and strode back toward the school.

"Alright, everyone," said Markham. "Half in one bus. Half in the other."

Sofia grabbed my hand and we were off. Zane, Kai, Paisley, Ciara, Eric, and I took up the middle rows for the six-hour drive. We had a great time laughing, joking, and passing around snacks until sleep claimed all of them but me.

I was wide awake when the bus turned onto the snow-shoveled lane and the resort opened up before us. It was even more beautiful than the brochure suggested. The massive brown structure boasted so many large windows I knew I would have my choice of places to sit out and watch the sun rising over the snow-capped mountains.

Something I would love to do with my boys... if the threat of Ace didn't hang over my head. Darkness tinged my happy mood. *The sooner we take them down, the better.*

The bus rumbled to a stop before the sliding doors so I roused Sofia. We were subdued and half-asleep as we gathered our bags and followed Markham into the resort. She pelted us with a steady stream of instructions as she led the way.

"Breakfast is from seven to nine. Lunch is at noon. Dinner is from six to eight. Be on time. Ski lessons are available for beginners and the more experienced are free to go out as they like, but do not take on more than you can handle. I have no desire to tell a parent their child broke their neck because they were messing around on the slopes.

"Girls will be on the first floor and the boys will be on the second. Different genders are not to go into each other's rooms. I have copies of all room keys and I will be making surprise visits." She peered over her shoulder to glare at us. "I'm certain we will have no problem in that arena. Correct?"

"Yes, Professor."

"Excellent. Then grab a roommate, a key, and a suite. It's been a long day. Get some rest."

Sofia snagged us the best suite at the end of the hall. My jaw dropped when we went inside.

"Sof, this is amazing."

"You think so?" She poked her head into the bedroom. "I guess it's okay. They only have queen-size beds though."

I heaved a sigh. "I forget how much of a snob you can be."

"Hey, watch it, Moon." Sofia darted into the bedroom. I shrugged, surprised that she had dropped it so easily.

"So what's first on the—"

"Ah ha!" Sofia burst into the doorway. I only had time to shriek before the pillow came hurtling at my head. It smacked me square in the face to the sound of Sofia's howling.

I threw my bag down. "That's it!"

She screamed as I ran into the bedroom and dove for the mountain of pillows on my bed. What followed was the pillow fight to end all pillow fights. It only stopped when Markham burst into our room, found us guffawing in a heap on the floor, and ordered us to bed.

This was already a great trip, and it would only get better.

"SO THIS IS IT. WE'RE doing this. We're really doing this. This is it."

With difficulty, I peeled my eyes off of Maverick. He looked delicious in a tight ski jacket and fitted jeans. He was going out to ski for real with the other guys while Kai and I hit the beginner lessons.

I shifted my attention to my friend and tried not to laugh. Kai stabbed at his bacon and eggs without managing to get any of it in his mouth. He looked like he was about to run.

"Why are you so nervous?"

He gave me a crazy look. "I'm about to hurtle down a mountain with two pieces of wood strapped to my feet. Why aren't *you* nervous?"

"I doubt there will be much hurtling. We'll probably be learning how to walk and stop first."

He threw down his fork. "This is a bad idea."

I laughed. "If you want to skip it and watch more movies in the rec room, I'm game. The kitchen makes caramel popcorn on demand."

"No." Kai took an exaggerated breath. "No, we'll do it. Never let it be said that Kai Thomas was afraid."

"As opposed to yesterday when you screamed like a six-year-old during the movie?"

"That was your fault! You came for me just when the killer popped out!"

"I tapped you on the shoulder and asked if you wanted pizza!"

"Exactly! You knew what you were doing."

By then I couldn't take it anymore and fell out laughing. After a minute, Kai joined in and soon the rest of the room was looking at us—including the Knights.

I spotted Jaxson's scowl across the tables. He was less than pleased that I was eating breakfast, skiing, and watching movies with Kai while we hadn't been able to find a single moment alone together. Markham made good on her threat to pop in on us. She even woke me and Sofia up in the wee hours of the morning checking to make sure our boyfriends hadn't made a visit.

If that wasn't bad enough, there was no privacy in the resort. Students popped in and out of the rec room, sauna, pool, and kitchen—all places we had tried to meet up. Three days in and it was looking hopeless.

"Come on," I said when I caught my breath. "Let's finish up and get out there. I'm sure it'll be fun."

"I'm holding you to that. If it's the disaster that I know it will be; I choose the movie tonight."

"Deal."

I stood and followed him out feeling happier than I had in a while. It was great being in sync with him again.

Kai and I stepped out of the resort and spotted the beginner group right away. Claire and her boyfriend, Ethan, waved us over. Things were still weird between Claire and me, but she spent most of her time studying and hanging out with Ethan so there was never a time to hash it out—and I wasn't starting now.

"Hi, Claire," I said lightly.

"Hey, Val."

We left it at that.

The instructor walked us through the first steps of choosing our skis, putting them on, and learning how to walk in them. Kai messed up on each one. He whacked a poor girl in the head when he chose his skis, fell over trying to put them on, and waddled around the snow while I openly laughed at him.

"You suck at this, Thomas," I shouted. "Use your poles!"

"Ima use them alright! Wait till I get over there, Moon."

"See you in a few hours."

Kai ripped off his glove just so he could flip me off and I laughed even harder. Unlike him, I was doing well. I carefully propelled myself through the snow like the instructor taught us.

"Very good, guys," the instructor called. "Now I'm going to show you the proper way to hold your skis—"

"So you don't hit anyone!" Tanya Leggot threw Kai a withering glare. The bruise on her forehead was turning purple.

"—and then that will conclude the session," he finished.

I twisted around to poke at the lever for the bindings. My left foot popped free and I moved to my right. I jabbed at the lever and tugged.

My foot didn't budge.

I pressed harder, but the binding didn't loosen.

"Val, what's wrong?"

"I can't get my foot out." I jerked my leg. "The binding is stuck."

"Wait, hold on." Kai stepped around me and took hold of my thigh. "Push while I pull."

I jammed down with the poles while he yanked on me. We both groaned with the effort.

"Shit, you're really in there." Kai shifted and put his arm around my waist. He pressed me to his chest and then put my free leg between his while he got a firmer hold on the other.

"You two," I heard the instructor call. "What's the problem?"

"Ready?"

"Okay."

"Now."

One hard pull and I popped free. The poles shot out of my hands as the force knocked me off-balance.

"Ahhh!"

Kai and I collapsed to the ground in a shower of white powder. I fell on top of him, and from the groans, it was none too gently. Shouts went up around us as I pushed myself up on my elbows.

"Are you okay?" Kai's body was a hard mass beneath me. I felt along his chest to check him. "Did I hurt you?"

"Moon," he wheezed.

"Yes?"

"I'm definitely picking the movie tonight."

"HERE YOU GO, KAI." I leaned over the back of the couch and wiggled his plate in his face. "Cheese pizza with green onions and red pepper flakes."

The guy took his eyes off the television to accept his prize. "Thank you."

A snort pulled our eyes to the right. Zane and Sofia shared the same armchair. She sat securely in his lap while he whispered things in her ear that was making her turn red.

"You don't have to wait on him, Val. You know he lied about you bruising his rib so he could get out of ski lessons."

"Hey, man," Kai cried. "Whose side are you on? We shared a womb."

"It's cool, Zane. I'm letting him have this one." I patted Kai's shoulder before straightening. "I'm going to the sauna. Muscles I didn't know I had are sore."

"Want me to come with you?" Sofia offered.

"No, it's alright." I winked at her. "You and Zane continue your talk."

I went back to our room and changed into a simple cotton wrap provided by the resort. I was really starting to get used to the luxurious life my friends and boyfriends led. It's been saunas, hot tubs, and imported cocoa by the fireplace every night I'd been here.

The resort sauna was a charming space—nothing like the claustrophobic cardboard boxes I had seen in the movies. Red and gold mosaic tiles covered the walls and there were three levels for people to steam on.

I stretched out and let my eyes flutter shut as the heat rolled over me. I lay there for so long, I had slipped into a doze when the sound of the door opening roused me.

"I'm sorry," I said as I rubbed my eyes. "Do you want to be alone? I can head out."

"No, I want to talk to you."

I snatched my hands away but looking only confirmed it. Ezra stood fully dressed in front of the door.

"What are you doing in here?" I swung my legs onto the floor. "Markham will freak if she finds us in here together."

He didn't reply. Ezra's expression was one I didn't know. Obsidian eyes tracked me as I got to my feet and closed the distance between us.

"What's wrong?"

"What's wrong?" Something flashed in his dark orbs. "You told me there was nothing going on with you and Thomas."

I blinked. "There isn't."

"Then what's this?"

Ezra lifted his phone. On the screen were two photos of me and Kai embracing as he grasped my legs, and then the other of me on top of him in the snow, laughing away. To anyone else, these pics told a guilty story.

"This is— This is nothing!" I snatched it out of his hand. "Who sent you this? Was it Ace? I can't believe they—"

"It wasn't Ace." Ezra's voice was hard. "It was Natalie."

I heaved a groan. "Ugh, that bitch never quits. Why would you worry about anything that comes from her, Ezra? She spouts nothing but bullshit."

"Doesn't look like bullshit." The heat was collecting on his forehead in beads of sweat. He breathed deeper from the mix of the room and the anger I felt bubbling within him. "What were you doing on top of him?"

I folded my arms. "My foot got stuck, he helped me get out, and then we fell over in the snow. That's it. Kai and I are just friends, and you"—my hands flashed out and shoved him against the door—"have nothing to be jealous about."

Ezra growled low in his throat as he gazed at me through narrowed eyes. He was breathing harder than ever. Sweat ran down his face, glistening in the soft light of the room. Ezra looked like he was a hair away from exploding... and it was turning me on like crazy.

"But"—a slow smirk spread across my lips—"the truth is I kind of like you jealous."

He raised one perfect eyebrow. "Do you?"

"Oh yeah." I pressed my body against him as I draped my arms around his shoulders. "You're insanely sexy when you're mad, Ezra Lennox." I pressed a kiss to his jaw. "I see why you keep this side of you locked away." Another kiss. Then another. "But not with me. Never hide from me." My lips found his and the anger was unleashed.

Ezra gripped my ass hard as he lifted me. We fell on the wooden platform, already tearing at each other's clothes like they burned.

Ezra and I hadn't had sex yet, but it wasn't for lack of trying. At that moment, all I could think was that the wait was finally over. Then he loosened my wrap and I stopped thinking all together.

I hadn't put on any underwear beneath my wrap. As I straddled him naked as the day I was born, our lips clashed in a fiery duel as I pulled his belt free and threw it over his shoulder. His zipper I ripped apart as I stuck my hand through the lining of his boxers.

"Oh, fuck." Ezra's head fell back, breaking our kiss. His eyes glazed over in the heat of pleasure and steam and it spurred me on. "Dammit, Val."

"Do you have a condom?"

Ezra snapped his head up as his eyes cleared. He gave me a look that said it all.

It was like an icy bucket of water had doused us.

"I'll— I'll go get one."

"Ezra, how could you not have a condom?" I asked as I pulled my hand out.

He threw his hands up. "I came here to confront you about Thomas. I didn't think this was going to happen, did I?"

"We're probably not going to get a chance like this again." I clambered off of him and reached for my wrap. "No Markham. No Ace. No moms."

"I'm sorry." Oh boy, did he sound it. Ezra took my hand after I got dressed and pulled me back onto his lap. "It'll happen." He glanced around. "And when it does, it'll be somewhere better than this."

"I'm starting not to care where it is, I just want to be with you." I leaned into his chest. "If I knew confessing to your mother would have such an effect on our sex life."

He sighed. "Tell me about it."

The two of us had gotten our weekend pass and went to see Ezra's mom. Confessing the truth of what happened the night of the football game had been hard, but facing her reaction had been even harder. She alternated between yelling at me and yelling at Ezra for the spring break video that started it all. Then she started crying which was even worse.

I went back to school while Ezra stayed with his mom. When he came back, he told me she had settled on mad. It was difficult to punish him when he lived at the school, but she was doing a pretty good job by denying permission for every weekend pass he asked for, and with us having to be careful at school, we had no chance to be together.

"Any chance your mom will ease up?"

"Maybe after break." Ezra ran his fingers through my growing hair. The act soothed my frustration until I was relaxed and warm once again. My Ezra was dark and possessive, but I always felt safe in his arms. "She's bringing me to New Zealand so I think she's thawing."

"I can't believe you're all going away."

"We'll be back, and we'll talk every day." Ezra tugged on my short strands until I tilted my head back. He pressed his lips to my—

Bang!

I fell out of his arms and hit the ground with a thud.

"Hello? Who's in here?"

I don't think I ever moved so fast in my life. The two of us scrambled to fix ourselves as the footsteps grew louder. We burst out just as Markham reached the door.

She blinked at the sweaty out-of-breath pair we made. "What is this? What were you two doing in there?"

"I was just—"

"Nothing—"

"We were looking for—"

"Val lost her—"

"That's right. I lost my—"

"And I was helping her look—"

Markham's eyes ping-ponged between the two of us as we stammered out excuses. The wrinkles on her forehead became more pronounced as she crossed her arms. "Miss Moon lost her what exactly?"

"My— My earrings," I blurted. "I lost them earlier and Ezra was helping me look."

She lifted a brow. "You don't wear earrings into a sauna."

I forced a laugh. "I know that for next time."

She harrumphed. "That's enough of this foolishness. Mr. Lennox, get back to your room now."

Ever the good boy in public, Ezra took off without argument. I tried to follow him.

"Miss Moon, a word."

I stopped. "Yes, Professor?"

"Walk with me."

She let Ezra go on ahead and then headed for the door at a slower pace. I fell in step beside her. Markham didn't speak right away. She kept her eyes fixed ahead as we walked through the halls in the direction of the lobby.

"Professor," I spoke up, finally breaking the silence. "Is something wrong?"

"You have done something unheard of, Miss Moon."

I made a face. "What? Lost my earrings?"

She didn't acknowledge that. She didn't even turn to look at me. "You have gone against the traditions of this school and won."

So it was this kind of conversation. I wrapped my arms around myself as we stepped out into the lobby. I was suddenly wishing I was wearing more than a thin piece of cotton.

"That was all I could do," I replied. "I wasn't leaving or backing down."

I didn't have to beat around the bush. The lobby was empty. The resort had gone to bed.

"I admire that; I do."

I gave her a hard look. "Your admiration means very little. The last two years have been hell and I couldn't rely on the people who were supposed to help me. Some of you were just as bad or worse." Visions of Scarlett flashed through my mind.

She remained expressionless. "You have every right to be angry—"

"Damn right, I do."

"—but it will change nothing," she finished. "If you think that Evergreen will become a better place now; you're mistaken. And if you think 'searching for earrings' with Mister Lennox means he won't turn on you again..."

I flushed at the implication.

"...then you are mistaken about that as well."

"That's not going to happen. It's over. The mark is lifted."

"The Knights are not the ones who get to say when it's over. They have their place and they were put there to uphold the traditions, not go against them. Quae sequenda traditio."

"Tradition is everything." I shook my head. "I don't understand this tradition of driving people out by any means necessary. Why do this? How did it even start?"

"It's been like this from the beginning."

"But who started it? Why?" I stepped up to her. "Is this about the Spades? What do you know about them?"

Her expression changed. Markham's face grew tight as her eyes narrowed to slits. "That is not a name you say out loud."

"Why? I get why people are afraid of them. I know what they've done and tried to do to me, but I don't understand how they started. Why are they allowed to run around doing this to people?"

"There is so much you still don't know."

"You're right. I *don't* understand why everyone doesn't fight back? Find them. Stop them."

She tossed her head. A frown marred her face, speaking to her agitation. "He used to say the same thing."

"Who would?"

Markham didn't seem to have heard me. "You can't stop who you can't see. Nora accepted that."

"Nora?" The name tugged a memory loose. "Do you mean Nora Wheatly?"

Markham's gaze sharpened. I suddenly had her full attention again. "How do you know that name?"

"I know she was marked, and that she was Walter McMillian's girlfriend. Is he who you were talking about?"

She eyed me. "You are aware of more than I thought."

"Yes, I am. Now tell me what you're *aware* of. For once, the truth."

"The truth will do nothing for you." Watching her face as closely as I was, I saw a flicker of emotion light in her eyes for the barest second: pain. "The truth did nothing for them."

"But, Prof—"

"Go to bed, Miss Moon." Markham straightened. "And I better not catch you in a similar position again."

I thought about arguing, but the look in her eyes told me that wouldn't get me far. I turned away and left for my room. Sofia stirred when I stepped into the bedroom.

"Val?" She stared blearily at me over the covers. "What's going on? Everything okay?"

I sighed as I climbed into my bed. "Every time I think I have things figured out; I discover how wrong I am."

"What does that mean?"

A wave of exhaustion washed over me. At that moment all I wanted to do was sleep and forget about secret societies, plots, and unsolved murders. "I'll tell you about it in the morning, okay."

"Okay."

I flicked out the lights and burrowed into the covers. Despite my feelings, all my worries followed me into my dreams.

"YOU'RE SAYING MARKHAM knew Walter?"

"Yes." I picked up a plate and handed it to Sofia. We were the only ones on the buffet line which gave me a chance to talk to her. "Not just that, but she knew Nora as well. I've been thinking that they must have gone to school together."

"You could be right. Markham is the right age. She would have been in her teens when everything went down with Walter."

I kissed my teeth. "It's impossible to look up anything about the Evergreen teachers—which is kind of disturbing. They have their official bios on the website and articles praising their accomplishments, but nothing about who they are or where they come from."

I knew this very well from all the trouble Maverick, Alex, and I have had trying to hunt down information on Scarlett.

"Well, we can find out if she went to school there easy enough," Sofia replied. She casually spooned scrambled eggs on her plate. "We just need a yearbook."

I gaped at her. My plate slipped through frozen fingers and clattered onto a pan of bacon.

"Val? What's up?"

"I'm an idiot," I whispered. "I am such a freaking idiot!"

She stared at me wide-eyed. "Um, okay. What are you talking—"

I grabbed her arms. "Yearbook, Sofia. Yearbook! Scarlett had a yearbook. She showed me Nora and Walter. She told me her father went to school here too."

"Scarlett? You mean the old art teacher?"

Sense quickly returned, sounding a warning. Sofia didn't know about Scarlett and it needed to stay that way. I pulled back. "Yes. She let me see the yearbook from that time, but I didn't think to look at anyone else."

"It'll be gone now," Sofia replied, confirming what I thought. "They cleaned out her class after she resigned."

I snapped my fingers. "What about the library? I bet they have..." I trailed off at Sofia's headshake.

"Other students had the same idea to look up Walter McMillian, the boy the Spades made an example of, but they don't keep copies of the yearbooks in the library. You can't find anything like that on campus."

"But... that's weird, isn't it? Why wouldn't they have copies?"

"I don't know but leave it to me. I'll find one."

"How are you going to do that?"

She smiled as she picked up my plate. "Just trust me."

We turned our attention back to the food as the doors opened behind us. I glanced over Sofia's shoulder and barely stifled a groan.

Please, don't start this early in the morning.

"Hey, Val." Natalie grinned at me as she, Airi, and Isabella reached for their plates and forks. "Did you like my photos? I sent it to everyone so they could see you're still open for business—slutting it up for the whole resort to see."

"You sent it to everyone so you could look even stupider than you normally do. Kai was helping me and we fell over. That's it. The real question is why you're following me around with your camera out. Do you know how creepy that is?"

Natalie's smirk didn't fade. "Maybe I'm waiting for the right chance to get you like you got me." She glanced up. "Nice hair, by the way."

My eyes narrowed. "What's that supposed to mean?" I surged forward. "Did you—"

"Val, stop." Sofia darted into my path. "She's not worth it."

She pulled me away over the sound of their laughter. I sat down and forced myself to eat as the dining room filled up. Evergreen students took up all the tables, and in the back by the professors, the Knights claimed a table for themselves.

"I'm never skiing again." I jumped as Kai slammed his plate down. "So we'll have to find something else to do, Moon."

I forced myself to look away from Ezra and focus on Kai. "What if I don't want to do something else? I didn't suck at it nearly as much as you."

"Come on. If I don't hang out with you, I'll be stuck with this guy." He leveled a finger at Zane as he took the seat next to Sofia. "Don't do that to me."

I rolled my eyes. "Why do you guys act like you're not best friends? You laugh and joke together more than me and Sofia."

"I love the guy like a brother—"

"He is your brother."

"—but you can only put up with him for so long." A biscuit went whizzing at his head and bounced off his nose. "See what I mean?"

"Why don't we all do something together?" I glanced at Sofia. "What do you have left on your list?"

"There's sledding, building a snowman, having a snowball fight, and chilling in the hot tub."

"Hot tub." The boys answered so fast I swatted both of their shoulders.

"What?" Kai laughed. "Sofia suggested it, not me."

"We can do the other stuff first," I said. "Then tonight we'll hit the hot tub with drinks and music."

"Won't Markham have a fit if she catches us?" asked Sofia.

"It'll be a group of us—boys and girls. It's not like we're going to have an orgy."

Kai inclined his head. "Although—"

Whack!

The guy guffawed as he protected his arm from more beatings. Yep, he was definitely back to his old self.

In my pocket, my phone vibrated. I took it out and looked at the screen. My good mood blew away like dust in a storm.

Ace.

I spared my laughing friends one more glance then smoothed out my face. I didn't want them to think something was wrong.

Ace: Looks like you're having a good time, but I hope you haven't forgotten about me.

I raised my head. Through my lashes, I looked around taking note of everyone who was in the room and on their phones. Almost all of the junior class and our professors had come down to breakfast. A phone was in nearly every hand.

Buzz. Buzz.

Ace: Looking for me? Well, I'm here. Let's see if you can find me.

My fingers flew across the screen.

Me: How about we stop playing these games? Tell me who you are.

Ace: Why would I do that?

Me: You wouldn't do that because you're a coward. You know it won't end well for you if I ever find your bitch ass. You want me to be afraid of you, but the truth is, you're afraid of me.

I waited for the reply. A minute passed. Then another. Then five more and nothing came.

"Val, you ready?" asked Sofia. She, Zane, and Kai picked up their empty plates to go.

"Yes, I'm ready."

I put my phone back in my pocket and joined my friends—leaving the lurking shadow of Ace behind.

THE FOUR OF US WERE having so much fun it got noticed. Our shrieks brought attention to our snowball fight and soon Eric, Ciara, and Paisley joined in. It was like nothing ever happened between us as we raced our sleds and challenged each other on who could build the best snowman. Sofia and I beat out Kai and Zane by a mile.

"You guys are doing the hot tub with us, right?" Kai asked. He threw an arm around my shoulder as we gathered in the lobby. "But I warn you, Val says no orgies."

Eric burst out laughing. "Damn. There goes my night."

I clapped my hand over Kai's face and playfully shoved him. "Ignore everything this guy says."

"I always do," Zane piped up.

The group laughed. Happiness was brimming so high I thought it would spill over. I wasn't ready for it to end either. "Join us. Sofia is going to get glasses and cider from the kitchen and I'm bringing my speakers."

"Can't pass that up," said Paisley. "I'll change and meet you guys down there."

Everyone else agreed and we broke up to go to our rooms. I changed into my bathing suit. It was a one-piece so not very scandalous, but it looked cute on me.

Sofia and I took up our towels and headed out. I went straight for the hot tub while she veered off to the kitchen. The folds of the fabric chimed just before I reached the room.

Maverick: Coleman came down with a cold and is laid up in his room. Felton is asleep and Ezra is off talking to his mom. If you come up now, we'll have the room to ourselves.

I stopped and looked back the way I came. That was tempting. So very tempting.

Me: I can't. I'm supposed to hang out with my friends. Besides, I've almost been caught once. Don't want to push my luck.

Maverick: We haven't spent any time together this whole trip. We should be watching movies together and sitting in front of the fire.

Me: I wish we could.

Maverick: I keep thinking about last weekend when we went to my place and

I stopped reading right there. I remembered vividly what we did at his place while his parents were out and if this kept up, I would give in and run up to his room. I avoided reading his message as I typed mine.

Me: We'll be together soon. I promise. Talk to you later.

Maverick: Bye. I love you.

Those three final words warmed me better than the hot tub ever would. I had yet to say it back to him, but I had a feeling the time was getting closer when it would be right.

I tucked my phone back into my towel and went inside. The hot tub was already bubbling from someone else's visit so I turned on the music and got in. It didn't take long for everyone else to arrive and soon we were laughing and goofing off over flutes of cider.

"Let's do truth or dare," Paisley asked.

I shook my head. "No way. I'm still traumatized from Isabella's party in freshman year."

"Then you'll have to pick dare this time."

"I don't think that will end any better for me."

Kai lifted a hand. "Hold up. What are we missing? What happened in freshman year?"

"You don't need to—"

"Everyone made Val answer the most embarrassing truths imaginable," Ciara piped up.

"You don't have to tell him," I cried.

Kai grinned. "I agree with Paisley then. It's all dare for you."

"Not when you have that look on your face."

He adopted an innocent expression immediately. "What? You don't trust me?"

"Not even a—" My phone chimed with a text. "One sec."

I wiped my hands on the towel before taking it out. My smile melted away when I saw who it was. The party went on around me as I opened the message.

Ace: I'm not afraid of you. Why would I be? I hold all the cards. But if you want to meet me that badly, you only had to say. Come out onto the terrace behind the rec room. If you're not there in ten minutes, I'm leaving.

I read the message once, twice, then a third time. Were they serious? They were finally going to reveal themselves? What do I do?

Go. This is my chance to end this. Find out what they want and what it will take to make that video disappear.

"Guys, I have to go." I picked up my things and clambered out to their protests.

"Go where?" asked Sofia.

"I left something in my room." I jammed my feet in my shoes and wrapped the towel tightly around me. "I'll be back soon."

I went into the hall dripping wet and not caring. The closed door muted the noise of my friends and plunged me into silence. I looked at my clock.

Seven minutes.

There was no time to find the Knights or make a plan. I had to get out there before Ace was gone. The sound of my flip-flops smacking on the hardwood echoed through the halls. I could hear people in the distance having a good time, but at that moment the lobby was empty except for a lone employee behind the desk. A thought entered my mind as I neared the rec room.

Tell the Knights. They can come and confront them too.

I had my phone out before I finished the thought.

Me: I'm meeting Ace on the terrace behind the rec room right now. I'm ending this.

I sent the message to all the boys and then stepped into the rec room.

The room itself was a small, cozy space, but the double doors at the back led to a beautiful wooden terrace perfect for sitting out and enjoying the sunset.

The sun was long gone when I stepped outside. Darkness covered the deck and the shadows cast by the balcony above made it even darker. I reached out and flicked the lamps on, piercing the gloom, and I saw one thing right away.

There was no one here.

Slowly, I walked further out. The terrace led down to a frost-covered garden and then on to the woods. I shivered. The cold whipped and bit at me, making goose bumps break out over my damp skin.

"Hello?"

A glance at my clock told me I still had four minutes left.

Where are they? I took another step toward the railing. *Are they in the garden?*

"Hello? Where are you?"

I peered over my shoulder, but there wasn't a soul in the rec room either.

This was a waste of time. They aren't com—

Pain exploded in my shoulder. I screamed as something came down on me hard. The surprise made my knees buckle, and my phone went flying as I fell.

The last thing I saw was the railing rising up to meet me.

Chapter Ten

" **...D**oesn't happen..."
       "...on purpose..."
"This was supposed to be over!"
The shout ripped me back to consciousness.
"Wha—?"
"Val?"
I peeled my eyes open and found a figure standing over me. It took a few seconds for my vision to clear. "Sofia?"

"Oh, Val." Concern was etched into every line of her face. "Are you okay? What happened?"

"I was going to ask you that." I tried to push myself up and cried out. My shoulder throbbed its displeasure. Looking around, I saw I was in the infirmary and we weren't alone. Markham stood next to a woman I assumed was the doctor. "What happened?" I repeated.

Markham stepped up to Sofia's side. "You were found last night on the terrace with a ski on top of you. There was a cut on your head from where you hit the railing so you were brought here immediately."

I gaped at her. *That bastard dropped a ski on me?!*
"What do you remember?"

I shifted my attention to the doctor. "Nothing. I didn't see anyone," I said honestly. "I was going back inside when I felt something hit my shoulder." Talking about it made it throb more. "What's wrong with it?"

"Your shoulder is fine, but you have a pretty nasty bruise," said the young brunette woman. "Your head is okay too. The cut is superficial and should heal without a scar. If you do show signs of concussion, come back to me. Otherwise, let's be thankful this accident wasn't worse."

"This wasn't an accident," Sofia snapped. I got the feeling it wasn't the first time. "Skis don't fall from the sky. Someone did this to her!"

Markham grasped her shoulder. "Miss Richards."

"This was supposed to be over. Why would anyone do this?"

"Miss Richards, that is enough." Her tone brokered no argument. "Val has had a long night and needs to rest. Help her to her room."

Sofia opened her mouth, but I stopped her with a hand on the arm. "I want to get out of here, Sof. Please, help me up."

She didn't argue anymore. Carefully, she put my good arm around her shoulder and helped me out of the room. I was still in my bathing suit.

"Where is my phone?"

"Jaxson has it. He was the one who found you."

"Okay. Can you get it back afterward? I want to—"

"I want to know what we're going to do about Ace."

The fury in her voice quieted me.

"I'm not stupid, Val. You got a text and then you went running out onto that terrace in your bathing suit. I know Ace attacked you."

"I know it too." I hugged her tighter. "What I don't know is who Ace is. There's nothing Markham can do."

"I bet it's Natalie." Sofia was practically vibrating with anger. "You heard her yesterday. She said she was stalking you and waiting for the right moment to get you back. She's gotten physical before."

I considered that as Sofia let us into the room. *Was Ace Natalie?*

"It could be her." Sofia set me down on the bed. I settled into the covers while she dug in my bag for a change of clothes. "But I don't know how we'd prove it. She's vicious, but she's not stupid. She won't admit it."

Still, I thought. *I'm keeping an eye on that chick. Airi and Isabella too. If this isn't about the Spades then it has to be someone who simply wants to take me down. They fit that description big-time.*

"If she did this, I'm going to do more than drop a ski on her head. Crazy bitch!" She ripped my top out of the duffle and my shorts got the same treatment. "And you!"

I sunk lower in the pillow when she leveled flashing eyes on me. "Me? What did I do?"

"Why would you go out there alone?!"

"Because I— Ace said they were going to reveal themselves. I thought it was my chance to end this once and for all."

"Dumbass!"

I goggled at her. "Sof!" Sofia had never yelled at me like this before.

"Don't 'Sof' me." She stomped over to me and lifted the blankets off. Her hands were gentle as she helped me out of the bathing suit, but her words were anything but. "That was such an obvious trap. Why in the hell would they tell you who they are and then meet you alone? So you could show up with your band of Knights and beat them into the snow? Who would be that stupid?"

"I see that now," I grumbled. "I was trying to provoke them and I thought it worked. Clearly, it didn't."

"They could have really hurt you, Val." The anger was fading and being replaced by an emotion that made me feel worse. Sofia's voice was thick with unshed tears. "You were almost *killed* more than once last year. You can't afford to make it easy for psychos to get you."

I caught her hand and held it tight. "Sof, I'm sorry. I should have told you what was going on and I definitely shouldn't have gone out there alone, but if it's worth anything, I don't think Ace is trying to kill me."

"How do you know that?"

"Dropping a ski on me hurt like hell, but there's no way that would have killed me. If they wanted to do that, there are plenty of heavier things around the resort that would have caved in my skull nicely."

She hissed. "Don't say that."

"It's true. If anything, that was punishment for trying to push their buttons. They told me not to make them angry, and now they showed me what they will do if I don't listen."

"This is really freaking me out." Sofia threw herself down next to me. I enfolded her in a hug as she fought tears. "We have to stop them. This needs to be over."

"We will." I rested my chin on her head. "One way or another, I will end this."

We sat there in silence for a while. A silence that was only broken by a knock on the door. Sofia stood up to get it.

"Hey, Val." Kai waved from the doorway. "Can I come in? Markham said it was okay if we left the door open."

"She needs to rest, Kai."

"There is something important I need to talk to her about."

I sat up a little straighter. *Is he here for what I think he is?*

"It's okay, Sofia. Let him in."

Kai came through and perched himself on the edge of the mattress. Sofia propped the door open with a chair and then left us alone.

"How are you doing?"

"I'm okay. My shoulder is a bit sore but the doctor said it was nothing serious."

"Everyone is talking about what happened, Val, and they are having a hard time believing a ski would fall from the sky on accident." He shook his head. "I was really freaked when I heard, and I realized it was past time that we talked."

I held my breath. This was it. I could feel it.

What am I supposed to say? I don't have those feelings for him, but I don't want to lose him again. How do I explain being blackmailed?

"Val, I want you to know how I feel."

I stiffened. I can't let him confess when I don't feel the same.

"I think we should just be friends—"

"I don't have feelings for you like—"

We both cut off, blinking at each other.

"Wait," I said. "Did you just say friends?"

"Yes. What did you say?"

"I said I don't have feelings for you like that."

"Really? Then... why did you kiss me at the homecoming dance?"

"I don't know. I guess I got caught up in the moment. Why did you kiss me back?"

He shrugged. "Because you're hot."

My foot shot out of the covers and shoved him off. He went down laughing.

"I'm serious," he said as he righted himself. "A smart, beautiful, funny girl kissed me. I wasn't going to run away screaming. But after it happened, I knew it was a mistake. I just didn't know how to tell you."

My relief was huge. The breath I had been holding whooshed out of me. "I'm so happy to hear you say that. You're my friend. One of the only people I can say never let me down. I didn't want to lose you."

He cracked a smile. "Nah. You're stuck with me for a bit longer."

"It's funny," I continued. "People swore up and down that you had a crush on me."

Kai's smile twitched. "Well, I kind of did at first. You remind me so much of her."

"Of who?"

"Thabisa."

Of course. The ex-girlfriend.

"She didn't take shit from anyone either. You even have the same laugh." He sighed. "But it's not the same. You're not her and now I've accepted that we're meant to be friends."

"I'm sorry, Kai." I closed my fingers over his hand.

"It's okay. Besides, I know you're still with the Knights and"—a grin broke out on his face—"I couldn't be a part of your harem. I'm not the kind of guy who can share."

"It's— It's not a harem!"

"Yeah? Then what would you call it?"

"It's— We— I mean, we're dating—"

He was laughing at me now.

Huffing, I flipped back into bed and pulled over the covers. "I'm tired. Go away."

Kai chuckled all the way out the door. The guy was too much sometimes but I was glad to have him back.

THE REST OF THE WINTER trip wasn't as fun after my forced visit to the infirmary. My friends stuck to me like glue when I was out of my room, and the Knights strolled the halls snapping at everyone for the smallest things. It was a relief when we finally rolled up at Evergreen Academy and I saw Mom's car waiting for me in front of the gates.

Olivia hugged me hard enough to squeeze out my stuffing.

"Hi, kid. It's so good to have you back. Did you have fun?"

"Yes, but I can't wait to be home."

"Me too. We see you so much more now, but I still miss you like crazy. Turns out I like you."

"After seventeen years it was bound to happen."

We laughed and piled into the car. I got into the back and leaned over Adam's seat to give him a kiss.

"Hello, baby."

His green eyes lit up and filled me with warmth. "Tina!"

"I missed you so much. It's just going to be the three of us this Christmas. No Sofia."

"Fia," he repeated. He looked at me curiously.

"But we're going to have fun."

Olivia pulled away from the curb and put Evergreen in her rearview.

"Mommy is going to make sure it's the best holiday ever."

I kept my promise. Mom lent me her car and I took Adam out every day. We went to the park, the zoo, the beach, museums, on picnics, the pet store—everything I could think of. Adam was well and truly on his way to being spoiled.

By Christmas Eve, all worries about Ace had fled. My only thoughts were about enjoying myself with my family.

It seemed everyone was enjoying themselves too. I got six texts from Maverick, Ezra, Jaxson, Sofia, Zane, and Kai wishing me a happy Christmas and giving me updates. There wasn't a word from Ryder.

I sighed as I looked across the tub. Adam shrieked as he played in my bubble bath.

"Why are boys so complicated? You won't be complicated, will you, Adam?"

His response was to grab his toy boat and fling it into the toilet.

"I'm taking that as a yes."

Knock. Knock.

"Hey, kid. You almost done in there? Someone is here to see you."

"Who is it?"

"Ryder Shea."

"Haha. Very funny. Seriously. Who is it?"

"Just finish up."

I did as she ordered and drained the tub. Adam was put in his baby robe while I wrapped myself in a fluffy towel. We stepped out into the hall toward the living room.

"Mom? Who is here? I—"

Ryder put down the drink Mom gave him and stood. "Hey, Moon." Ryder was dressed casually in a pair of jeans, shirt, and a light jacket. Simple, but somehow, he made it look like the latest fashion trend.

"What are you doing here?" I probably could have come up with a better opening than that but it was the first thing to come to mind.

"If you're not busy, I wanted to take you out." He glanced at Adam. "Both of you."

"Take us out? Why?"

"I still have a lot of apologizing to do."

"But it's Christmas Eve. Don't you want to spend it with your mom."

"Mom is resting today." He peered over his shoulder at Olivia. "Do you mind if we go?"

"Nope. Take her. Take them both. We were going to go to Santa's Village today, but you three can do that."

"Alright."

It seemed it was decided.

Ryder turned back and looked me up and down. "I'll wait for you to get dressed."

I didn't argue. I went into my room and got us both ready. Ryder was waiting outside for me when I came out with my son and diaper bag.

"Your mom put the baby seat in my car so we can leave when you're ready."

"We can go." I took in the shiny red ride sitting in my driveway. "No driver today?"

"No. Just us."

Three simple words and they burrowed straight through me. Why shouldn't they? They were ones I had never heard him say. *Just us.*

I tried to ignore the bubbles bursting in my stomach as I buckled Adam in. I took my place in the front seat and we set off.

The ride to the village was quiet except for me giving him directions, and by the time we got there I was fighting my nerves.

What are we doing? Ryder and I have never done anything like this before. We've never had a moment alone that didn't end in disaster. What do we even talk about?

I fretted all the way through parking and joining the ticket line. *How do I do this?*

"I can help you."

I pulled out of my whirling thoughts. "What?"

Ryder accepted the tickets then stepped out of line. "I'll help. Do you want me to hold Adam or the diaper bag?"

"No, I'm fine. I don't need help."

"You're ridiculous sometimes, Moon."

There was just no smoothing out that prickly personality, but to his credit, I did hear a trace of fondness.

Ryder put out his hands. "Come on."

I sighed. "Alright. Thanks. You can take the diaper bag."

He moved in and Adam seized his chance. The baby twisted out of my hold and fell into his arms.

"Adam, no—"

Ryder scooped him up and turned to go without a word. Over his shoulder, Adam peered back at me looking pretty pleased with himself. "Tina."

I sighed. "I'm coming, baby."

Together we passed through the gates into the winter wonderland. I loved this place. This far south granted us all the biting chill without the snow, but they had managed to make it festive. Hot foods, horse-drawn wagon rides, fake snow raining down, pictures with Santa, and Christmas lights. It was perfect.

"What do you want to do first?" I asked.

Ryder smiled down at me. "Whatever you want to do."

My breath caught. *I wonder if that smile will ever stop having this effect on me.*

A cry from Adam tore my eyes away. The baby pointed to the large animal pulling the wagon.

"Or maybe whatever Adam wants to do."

I chuckled. "We can do the wagon ride. Then we'll get a picture with Santa."

We kept going. This time in search of the line for the attraction. Once again, we lapsed into silence and it pressed on me.

What do we talk about? I thought as we joined the line. *I don't know how to have a normal conversation with Ryder Shea.*

Just think of something, another voice countered. *Anything!*

"So what have you done during the break?" I blurted. "Did you go anywhere? See anyone?"

"Mom wanted to stay home," he replied easily. "Except for swinging by Maverick's to get her present, I haven't left the house until today."

"What did you get her?"

"A kitten."

I perked up. "Really? Maverick's kittens? Was it Penelope or Preston?"

"Penelope. But I changed her name."

"You didn't like it? I gave them their names."

"And you went with Penelope and Preston?"

"Hey, it fits. They were both born at a snobby prep school. They should have snobby rich kid names."

A ghost of a smile appeared on his lips. "You mean like Ryder? How does that fit into your stereotype?"

"I mean like Charles," I shot back. "Your actual middle name."

He winced. "Okay, point taken, but I'd say yours is included, *Blythe*."

"Never say that name again."

Ryder threw his head back laughing. After a second I giggled along too. *This is amazing. We're actually vibing.*

The line moved so we inched up. "What did you name her?"

"Valentina."

I gaped at him. "Really?"

Ryder took one look at me and lost it. "No, not really," he said between laughing.

"Not cool." I whacked him upside the arm.

Ryder ducked. "Hey, you can't hit me. I've got a baby."

"Then hand him over."

"Not a chance."

We were still laughing as the attendant waved us up to the wagon. I climbed up first and scooched over for the boys.

"Ready, Adam?" Ryder asked. He got the toddler in both hands and began swinging him. "One. Two. Three!" Adam squealed with laughter as Ryder swung him back and forth then popped him up on the seat.

The sight of them together loosened something within me. "You're good with kids," I said as Ryder took his place next to us.

"You sound surprised."

"Of course, I'm surprised. Before everything went down you were as warm as a glacier. Babies don't go for that stuff."

"I always did like how you told it as it is." His tone was light despite my remark. "My mom has a friend who comes by to visit her on her good days. She brings her kids and they hang off of me like tree ornaments. Sylvia and her kids make Mom laugh. I wouldn't be cold to them."

"You really love her." The words fell from my lips before I could stop them. Even I could hear the tone of surprise.

Frowning, Ryder visibly stiffened. "She is my mother, Valentina. How dead inside do you think I am?"

"No, I— That didn't come out right. I meant it's sweet how much you both care about each other. I hope Adam and I are that close when he's a teenager."

It was slow, but as the wagon rumbled down the path, he relaxed. "You will be," he finally said. "The kid is in love with his Tina. Anyone can see that."

"You think so?" I whispered. I reached out to smooth Adam's curls. "I hate how much time I spend away from him. Mom calls me at least once a week to talk to him because he's crying for me."

"You're doing this for him." Something in his voice made me meet his eyes. "He'll understand that."

Usually there was nothing to see in those silver orbs, but at that moment, I saw everything I needed to know. "Thank you."

The horse cantered around the village, showing us the beautiful sight of Christmas trees and happy people. At some point during the ride, Ryder draped his arm over the seat behind me. He didn't touch me, but still I felt his warmth against my back. I felt it stronger as I drifted nearer to him. Even with Adam between us, I never felt closer to him.

How did he know that this is what I really wanted for his labor?

The wagon dropped us off at our original stop. I picked up Adam before he could reach for Ryder. "Nope. Mommy's got you now." The baby giggled like making me jealous was a part of his plan. "Next stop: Pictures with Santa."

"Sounds good," Ryder replied. He offered me a hand to help me down.

"I should warn you. Adam and Santa have a shaky relationship."

"What does that mean?"

"It means," I said as I led the way. "That he has screamed the place down both years that he's been on that man's lap. We're hoping number three goes better."

"But Adam seems cool with strangers."

"Not when they're dressed in red and sporting oversized beards."

We got lucky that the line for pictures was short. Every year they outdid themselves with the decorations for Santa's workshop. This year was no different. Behind Santa's throne stood a massive gingerbread house with gumdrops so lifelike I could eat them. The big man himself perched on the platform smiling at the families that came before us.

That smile disappeared into his beard when he saw us. "Ah... you're back."

I pinked as Ryder stifled a laugh behind me. "He's older now. He'll be okay." I carefully handed over the toddler then backed away. "Alright, Adam. Just look at Tina. Smile for Tina."

Adam's tiny forehead wrinkled as he looked at my waving hands and beaming smile. He gazed at me, then up at the man staring down at him. When he looked back, his face crumpled.

"No, don't cry," I said desperately. "Come on, Adam. Smile."

"Look over here!" To my shock, Ryder had joined in. He jumped up and down next to me, making funny faces at the baby. "Smile, Adam."

We straight up looked ridiculous—bouncing around and pulling faces like lunatics. The people in line laughed at us. *I* laughed at us.

Adam did not laugh. He burst into ear-piercing screams that echoed through the village. Santa tried to save the photo.

"Come on, Adam." He twisted the baby on his knee to face him and began bouncing him up and down. "Tell Santa what you want for—"

Whack!

My jaw dropped. Adam had reeled back and smacked the jolly man across the face.

"Adam!"

Ryder doubled over—howling so loud he competed with Adam. I sprung forward and snatched my kid off the dumbfounded man's lap. I never moved so fast in my life.

"Let's go," I cried as the people in line laughed. I snagged Ryder's jacket. "We need to get out of here as fast as possible."

We booked it out of the workshop, racing through the crowd until my lungs cried out for me to stop. I pulled Ryder into a quiet corner between the candy apple and cider stands. There was barely any room. He leaned over me, only inches away, as we caught our breaths.

"I don't think they're chasing us." Traces of humor laced his tone.

"I wouldn't blame them if they were. We're probably banned for life after that."

"That was some slap."

Adam had quieted down. Gone were the tears, but a pout still hung on his lips. He wasn't impressed.

"You know." My gaze drifted back to Ryder. There was no smirk on his face. No chill in his eyes. The mask was gone and what lay beneath...

How could a mere mortal be this gorgeous? I felt like if I tried to touch him my hand would go right through. Ryder Shea cannot be real.

"This is the best Christmas Eve I've ever had. Thank you for coming out with me." Ryder lifted his hand and cupped my face. My pulse quickened as he gently brushed his thumb along my cheekbone. "And I'm sorry, Val. I'll never forgive myself for the things I did to you."

"I know." My voice was barely a whisper. It was hard to concentrate. Ryder's face was coming closer. Our lips were closing the distance and I couldn't hear my thoughts for the pounding in my ears. "But what matters is... you're a different person now and... I like that person."

"You do?" His breath ghosted over my lips.

"Yes, I do."

The words were barely out of my mouth before the distance between us was gone. Ryder's lips pressed against mine and—

"Ahh!"

"Ow!"

Ryder ripped away and stumbled back into the stall. He gazed at Adam and his raised fist with round eyes.

"Adam!" I cried. "We do *not* hit. No hitting. Say sorry to Ryder."

"It's okay." Ryder smiled as he rubbed his cheek. "I deserved that one. I'd hit the guy trying to put the moves on my mom right in front of me too."

A flush came over me. *Put the moves on?*

"Let's go," he said. "See as much as we can before they find us and ban us."

Shaking my head, I followed him out. We quickly salvaged the day. Adam went back to being his happy self as we stuffed our faces and enjoyed the rides.

The sun had set on the village by the time we decided to head home. Adam snoozed on Ryder's shoulder and every time I looked at them, I smiled. This was the best Christmas Eve I ever had too.

"Hey, wait!"

I turned as a woman in an elf costume ran up to us. We had just passed by Santa's workshop.

"I've got your picture," she said. She grinned as she handed it over. "I got the exact moment the old man's glasses went flying. Priceless." She laughed herself sick as she strolled off.

"That settles it," I grumbled. "We're never coming back here again."

We didn't talk on the ride back to my house but I felt no need to break the silence.

Mom opened the door the moment we put our feet on the porch. She took Adam off my hands and whisked him away with a wink that made me blush.

"So..." I slowly turned toward him. "Today was fun."

He nodded. "It was."

I stepped closer. "It meant a lot to me. You being so great with Adam."

"I like him." Ryder took a step closer himself. "The kid has a solid right hook."

I let out a soft laugh as we moved in, bumping into each other's chests. I rose up at the same time he bent down.

"Wait."

I froze with our lips a hair apart. "Wait? Why?"

"We shouldn't do this." Those silver eyes swept over me. I saw the tortuous battle raging inside him. "I got caught up at the village, but I shouldn't have tried to kiss you. I want to make it up to you, Valentina, but we don't have the same history that you do with the other guys. I have no right to kiss you. I have no right to be with you."

I placed my hand on his neck when he tried to pull away. "Can I decide that for myself?"

Ryder reached up and closed his hand over mine. He placed one soft kiss on my forehead before placing my hand at my side.

I stood there on the porch long after he was gone.

Chapter Eleven

I kept the smile on my face as I waved Mom and Adam off, but it disappeared the second they did.

Another semester at Evergreen Academy.

Christmas vacation had been wonderful—even with that blip at the end with Ryder—and I loved the brief spell of peace. Ace hadn't texted me once the entire time, but now that I was back, I had no reason to think the stay of execution would continue.

"Valentina!"

I turned just as Sofia launched herself at me. We laughed as we hugged, squeezing each other like it had been years instead of a couple of weeks.

"How was your vacation?" she asked as she pulled back. Behind us the staff were gathering our things to take up to our dorms. "Tell me it was miserable even if it wasn't because mine was miserable."

"It was miserable."

"Thank you."

"What happened?" I hooked my arm through hers as we lazily made for the gates. "I thought you were liking England from your texts."

"I was until I found out why the Madame and Mister brought me out there. It turns out they were planning on going *alone* until they found out just how often I bring Zane back to the house when they're not there. They were afraid I'd spend the whole vacation with him." She scoffed. "You won't believe it, Val. They actually sat me down and gave me the sex talk and went on about not getting serious too soon. I'd be touched by their parental concern if it wasn't seventeen years too late."

I shook my head. "I'm sorry, Sof. If it is any consolation"—I looked around to make sure no was close by—"I'm not doing so hot on the parenting either. My kid beats up innocent Santas."

"Oh no. You didn't make him sit on Santa's lap again, did you?"

"He's older now," I said in my defense. "I thought he could handle it."

She laughed. "That actually does make me feel better." She hip-bumped me. "As does what I have to tell you. I spoke to Eric and he's going to let us come to his place this weekend."

"Okay. Why?"

"Because." Sofia grabbed my arm and led me to the fountain. The bubbling water covered up her voice for any listening ears. "His family has been going to Evergreen Academy since forever. They've got yearbooks, Val. Loads of them. I've seen them in his library. I didn't tell him that's why we wanted to come because I couldn't explain. But you could sneak away and check them out."

"Sofia, I might love you."

She brushed her hair over her shoulder. "You definitely love me. And I love you. That's why we're going to finally unravel this mystery of the Spades, Knights, Evergreen and all that's been going on in this place. If the person texting you is the Ace of Spades, we need to know as much about this secret society as they clearly know about us."

"Agreed."

She squeezed my arm. "I have to go meet Zane, but this weekend it's you and me. We're going to end this and you"—she gripped me tighter—"are going to be careful and tell me if anything happens."

"I will."

She kissed my cheek before heading off. I walked away from the fountain at a slower pace, lost in my thoughts.

Is this the Ace of Spades? Ryder made a good point that the person never mentions the Spades once.

They also wouldn't need to bother tormenting me, another voice spoke up. *They would have marked me again and let the rest of the students do it for them.*

And does the Ace of Spades exist? What would be their purpose if they do? To lead the band of psychos?

I let out a frustrated sigh. I hated that I didn't know where to start with this. Two and a half years and the Spades were still a mystery wrapped in shadows. I was no closer to understanding Walter McMillian's death or why he would be killed if he was as insignificant as Scarlett claimed. I didn't know who among us was an enemy.

Sofia is right. Whether they are involved or not, I need to know who they are and how to stop them.

I passed under the school arch and my phone went off. Mind on other things, I took out my cell and glanced at it. The name on the screen made me halt.

Ace: Welcome back, Valentina. We're going to have even more fun this semester.

I WAVED AT MRS. KHAN when I went in. "Morning."

She beamed. "Morning, dear."

I liked the people in administration. They were next to useless if you had a problem, but there were always smiles on their faces and they were nothing if not polite.

"I was hoping for a pass for tomorrow. Just for the afternoon."

The first week of the new semester passed in a haze of lectures and homework. The professors didn't ease us in. With standardized tests coming up and college applications to prep for, the juniors were feeling the pressure.

Eric was looking forward to the three of us going to his place the next day. He had us by the pool sipping virgin margaritas before we got there.

Mrs. Khan lost her smile. "Oh, I'm sorry, Val. But I'm not allowed to give you passes anymore."

I blinked. "What? But I haven't done anything."

"It's not my decision, dear. The headmaster says all passes you request must be approved by him. He is free now if you would like to speak with him."

"Yes, please," I forced through gritted teeth.

Evergreen didn't lift his head when I came in. "Hello, sir."

"Miss Moon. Here to request a pass I suspect."

"Yes." I didn't bother to sit down. "It's only for a few hours, not the whole weekend."

"Miss Moon." Evergreen raised his head and placed it on top of his steepled fingers. "I shall tell you now that there will not be a repeat of last semester."

I was careful to keep my tone respectful. "Did I do something against the rules? I asked for passes and they were granted."

"You left campus eight weekends out of fifteen. We like to allow juniors and seniors more freedom as you become adults, but this is a privilege not to be abused."

"All I did was go home to see my family."

And made a few pit stops with Maverick and Jaxson along the way.

"I can appreciate that it is tough to be away from loved ones. I too miss my family."

Family? Evergreen has a family?

My eyes flicked down to his bare finger. I had never seen a ring on that hand or a family photo in this office. I had assumed he was married to this school.

"But when I am here," he continued, "I give the academy my full attention and that is what I expect of my students. Going forward, weekend passes will be restricted to no more than three a semester for all upperclassmen."

Great. Everyone is going to love me when they find out I'm the reason.

"Then I would like to use my first one now," I stated. "I believe you'll approve, sir. I'm going to meet Eric Eden's mother and discuss Somerset University. She graduated from there and said she is happy to walk me through the application and possibly give me a recommendation."

Not all of that was a lie. Eric did mention that his mother went to Somerset when I brought it up.

"Somerset University?" Evergreen's hands fell away from his chin. "That is a fine institution, Miss Moon. You would do well there."

"I hope so, sir."

"Well, you are correct in that I approve of this use of your time." He rose from his chair. "You may have the pass."

I thanked him and left. I didn't let the anger show on my face until I was halfway down the hall.

Only two passes left and fifteen weekends to go.

No more seeing my son whenever I want. No more sneaking off with Jaxson and Maverick. Not to mention the time I've been desperately trying to carve out with Ezra.

Why did every semester at this school only seem to get harder?

"ALRIGHT. MY MOM IS home so steer clear of her."

Eric held the car door open for me to get out. His car was sweet with a capital S. A sleek silver Mercedes that tried to seduce me with its heated leather seats and smooth interior. I was one stolen key away from adding it to my harem.

"Why do we have to avoid her?"

Eric shot me a look as he put his key in the lock. "She's been cooking all these heart-healthy meals since Dad's heart attack and making everyone who gets near her be taste testers. She says she wants to take care of him so she's taken over lunch and dinner from our chef."

"Aww," cooed Sofia. "That's sweet."

"It would be if the woman could cook." He placed his hand over his chest. "I love her. She gave me life. But if you see her coming: run."

We cracked up as Eric threw open the doors. We made it three steps before a woman rounded the corner and appeared in front of us.

"Mom," Eric cried.

Her full lips curled into a smile. "Hello, sweetie. Introduce me to your friend." She zeroed in on me.

"This is Valentina Moon."

I stepped forward to shake her hand. Her resemblance to Eric was so strong there was no doubt she was his mother from her lips to the curve of her cheekbones to the shape and color of her eyes.

"My name is Helene. I'm happy to have you in my home."

"Your place is incredible. Like a castle."

"It's old and stuffy but we like it."

Those weren't the adjectives I would have chosen for this place. Out of all the mansions around Evergreen that I had the chance to visit, this was the biggest. This was *twice* the size of the biggest. Castle was right in that the mansion was made of a smooth gray stone and topped with turrets. The inside was even more breathtaking by their choosing to go with the theme and fill the place with antique furniture.

"We're just going to hang out by the pool, Mom," Eric broke in. "Get a break from the academy."

"A break after one week? It only gets more difficult from here, sweetie. I hope you're taking your studies seriously."

"Of course, I am. It's just a few hours."

"A few hours is all it takes." Helene's voice was the definition of measured, but I picked up the scolding.

"Yes, Mom."

Her smile returned. "You all go on. I'll bring you a snack in a little while."

"You don't have to," Eric said quickly. "I know you're busy. We can feed ourselves."

"I'm never too busy for you," she replied as she walked away. "Make sure you say hello to your grandmother before you leave."

Eric waved us on. "Sof, you guys get changed and I'll meet you by the pool. I'm going to tell the chef to sneak us something decent to eat."

Sofia turned on me the second he disappeared. "Okay, the library is down that hallway. Fifth door on the left. I spotted the yearbooks on the bookshelves in the back by the window. Let me show you where the pool is first so you can find us after."

"Okay."

Sofia took me through the sprawling manor and out to the pool. Making my way back to the library was tough. I turned down the wrong hallway twice before I finally ended up where we started. It was simple from there to find the fifth door hanging open on the left.

The library of Eden Manor was as impressive as the rest of the home—maybe more so. The bookshelves reached as high as the rafters. They were as large as the grand windows that cast light on the quiet place.

My feet were soundless on the hardwood floors as I made my way to the back by the windows. I had no trouble finding the yearbooks exactly where Sofia said. My fingers swept the spines as I went thirty-eight years in the past.

This is it. This is the one Scarlett showed me.

I pulled it down and flipped through until I found the sophomore class.

There they were. Nora Wheatly and Walter McMillian.

Now let's see if you went to school with someone I know.

I flipped back to the freshman class and began there. I squinted at every face and name. I was halfway through the sophomores when a flicker of recognition stopped me.

Elizabeth Fairchild.

This was her. A different last name and a younger face, but there was no doubt in my mind that I was looking at the girl who would become Professor Markham.

I lowered my hands as that hit me. Markham didn't only know them. She was in the same class as Walter and Nora.

Markham was there when she was marked. She might know why it happened. She might have joined in on running her out. Then there's Walter. That was the year one of her classmates was killed. She must know something about it.

I shook my head. I would come back to Markham. Right now, I needed to find Scarlett's father. Somehow that woman became a Spade. If we could find out more about her. We might understand why she was chosen.

Two years ahead of Walter. That's what she said.

I paged straight through to the "L" last names.

Lake. Laban. LaBarre. Landis. Leon.

That was it. No more last names that started with "L" and no LeBlanc. The only name that came close was LaBarre and she was a girl.

"Argh!" I burst out.

"Hello?"

I jerked. The yearbook slipped through my fingers as a creak sounded in the library. It was soon followed by footsteps.

Stupid! Why didn't I check to make sure no one was in here?

"Who is there?"

"I... um..." I trailed off as a woman appeared at the end of the row.

She squinted at me through round-framed glasses. "Who are you? What are you doing in here?"

The wrinkles lining her face and hair that was more white than brown told of her age. Even so the straight back, tailored pantsuit, and stern expression told me she wasn't one to mess with.

"I'm Valentina. I'm a friend of Eric's. Are you his grandmother?"

"I am. My name is Wilhelmina Eden." She approached, still eying me suspiciously. "Why are you in here by yourself?"

"I-I was just—" My eyes were drawn down to the book at my feet and hers followed. "I was curious about Evergreen in the old days. I hope it's okay that I looked."

Her frown smoothed out. "Of course, it is. They are here to be looked at after all. Have you met my son? Eric's father."

I shook my head.

"Surely Eric has told you all about him," she stated. It wasn't a question.

"Yes, ma'am. Graduated top of his class. Ivy League university. On the board of Shea Industries."

She inclined her head. "My son does cut an impressive figure. I see why you started with his yearbook."

"His yearbook?"

She picked up the fallen book and flipped to the page she wanted in a second. She turned the book toward me and pointed to a face at the bottom.

Andrew Eden.

Something jiggled loose as I took in Andrew's charmingly handsome face. "There was something else I heard about him," I began. "Eric told me his dad... was a Knight."

"That is correct." She answered so easily I was taken aback. I couldn't speak about this stuff with Olivia or anyone else in the real world. I forgot sometimes that the world around Evergreen was an entirely different place. "It is a mantle that my son wore proudly. He did his duty to ensure he honored our legacy and the legacy of the academy. As I did when I was a Knight."

Pride was the word I would have used. It was woven through her every word. My brows drew together as I looked at her. This wasn't what I came here for but I may still learn something.

"Do you mind if I ask you questions?"

"Not at all." She lifted her chin a little higher. The first smile since I met her formed on her lips. "Ask away."

"Why were you and your son chosen?"

"I told you, dear. Legacy. Every generation there has been an Eden at Evergreen Academy and there always will be."

"Every generation?"

"Oh yes. All the way back to when the school began. My great-great-great-great grandfather was in the very first class."

"Wow," I breathed. "So did you know you would be picked?"

"No one ever knows, but I had a strong inkling."

"It must have been hard."

"Hard?"

"Fifteen years old and expected to cut your hair and keep a school full of kids in line. Did you ever regret becoming a Knight?"

"Never." She replied before the question was fully out of my mouth. "Duty, dear. It is all about duty. One can whimper in the face of it or they can stand up and do what must be done. Evergreen is what it is today because of those that did not shirk their duty and we are all better for it."

"Did your son feel the same way?" The words fell from my lips before I could stop them. "About Nora Wheatly."

Her eyes narrowed. "Excuse me?"

"He was a Knight when she was marked. He was there when her boyfriend was killed trying to protect her. I can't imagine he enjoyed being a Knight then."

Her gaze sharpened. The silence stretched between us as I wondered if I had gone too far. When she finally spoke, her voice was soft.

"You know quite a lot about this." She closed the yearbook with a snap. "What did you say your name was?"

"Valentina Moon."

She hummed low in her throat as she returned the book on the shelf. "You speak plainly. I admire that. So I will do the same."

"Thank y—"

"Nora Wheatly was a common slut."

I choked. Of all the things I had thought she would say, that didn't come close.

"What?"

"She was a slut," Wilhelmina repeated. "She brought shame to herself and, more importantly, to the school. She couldn't be allowed to remain and she accepted that. It was that boyfriend of hers that couldn't. That is the truth but what happened to Walter McMillian was unconscionable. It never should have come to that." She looked me dead in the eyes. "But you can be sure of two things: my son played no part in that boy's death and, two, he did his duty."

I nodded for lack of a better thing to do.

"Do you have any other questions?" Her smile was gone.

"No. I should go find my friends."

Wilhelmina stepped to the side to let me pass without a word.

I found the bathroom and changed into my suit. Eric and Sofia were slurping their margaritas when I came out.

"What took you so long?"

There was no point in lying when Wilhelmina could tell him the truth. "I found the library... and your grandmother."

He winced. "Don't know what happened, but let me say sorry. She can be kind of intense."

"Kind of?" I said under my breath.

I sat down on the pool chair between them and accepted the glass Eric handed me. He leaned back with a pleased sigh. "Let's enjoy this, ladies. It only gets worse from here."

Why did I have a strong feeling he was right?

ERIC WAS RIGHT. THE first month of junior year flew by in a haze of college applications, essays, tests, practice tests, mock interviews, and tears—especially the last one. I guess even Ace was busy because their taunting texts switched from daily to weekly.

"Good morning, class." Professor Coleman tapped a key on his computer and the projector came to life. "As you know, advanced placement tests are coming up as well as finals and SATs. You have a lot to accomplish and you've been feeling the pressure of the accelerated curriculum, but pressure is good."

From the glares half the class—me included—were giving him, we didn't agree that pressure was good.

"You're going to face nothing but pressure and challenges as you move on to your final year of Evergreen and then university," he continued. "I would like to say that I am proud of all you accomplished, and you should be too. Give yourself a round of applause."

The claps came slow, but eventually the room gave in, filling the space with cheers while Coleman smiled indulgently.

"Now then," he said when we finished, "let's talk about the ten-page essay you have due in two weeks."

The groans were ten times louder than the applause. Coleman's smile didn't even twitch.

"The man is a sadist," I hissed to Kai. "I swear."

"No arguments here."

"Settle down, settle down." He flapped his hands until we quieted. "*The Picture of Dorian Gray* is a relatively short book. You'll analyze it for the standard elements with a partner."

Kai turned to me. "Okay. Let's break it up by—"

"Different partners," Coleman interrupted. "I will assign them now."

Coleman went through the list and predictably busted us up. Kai shot me puppy dog eyes as he got up and moved over to Natalie.

"Valentina Moon and Ezra Lennox."

I bit my lip to hide my smile as Ezra sat next to me.

He didn't. "Hey, Moon."

"Lennox."

He leaned in and put his mouth to my ear. "I'm looking forward to late-night study sessions in my room."

A shiver went up my spine. "There will be *a lot* of late nights."

I wasn't only feeling the pressure. I was feeling the sexual frustration. I had two more weekend passes left and I wanted to hang on to them for emergencies. Of course that meant I couldn't go off with the boys, and with Ace hanging over our heads we couldn't hook up here.

Ezra gave me a look that shouldn't be allowed in public. We would be expected to grab alone time now. I didn't want to shave my head again or wake up in the nurse's office so I wouldn't push them, but this Ace couldn't act against. We didn't pick the partners, Coleman did.

Ace seemed to agree since they didn't order me to do anything over the next week while we worked on our project.

"We can talk more about the main themes of the story," I said. "We could write pages about youth. Good vs. evil. Sexuality."

"That's a good idea." Ezra's breath was warm in my ear. Years later and here we were in the library again, studying while he whispered to me. "But don't say sex. I'm already losing my mind getting to be this close to you."

I bit down on my smile. He was making it almost impossible to get any work done.

"Why haven't we already?"

"Because," I said softly. I kept my eyes on the laptop. "We tried working in your room, started fooling around the second I got in the door, and didn't get a lick of homework done. I told you. Let's finish the project early and then we can spend the rest of our 'study time' doing whatever we want."

"That seemed like such a good plan when I agreed to it."

"It is a good plan." I scooted my chair back and smiled into hooded eyes. "I'm going to get that grammar book. I don't want to be marked down again for putting a comma out of place."

I left Ezra and wandered to the back. There were a bunch of us working on the paper under the dim lamps of the library. Kai caught my eye as I walked past his table. His eyes grew large. He reached for me like he wanted me to save him.

"What are you doing?" Natalie snapped from his other side. "Pay attention."

I shot him a supportive thumbs up and continued to the final stack. There was total silence back here. Not many people were eager to read up on grammar. I found four copies of the book I needed exactly where I expected it to be.

That was easy. The sooner we get the paper done, the sooner we can be together.

I reached for the textbook...

...and squeaked when an arm grabbed my waist.

"I've been thinking about the plan," Ezra growled.

The room became a blur as he spun me around.

"And I think the plan is terrible."

I didn't have time to form a response before his lips were on mine. I made a half-hearted attempt to pull away but was quickly swept under. There was a reason I had said no sex until after the project. The heat between Ezra and I was explosive. Our clothes started coming off the second we were alone. Being with him was like being struck by lightning—raw, powerful, natural, but also dangerous.

That electricity surged through my body as we feverishly kissed against the stacks. His hands didn't stay still. They roamed and explored my body until they reached my thighs and then slipped beneath my dress. His finger brushed me over the fabric of my underwear. We broke apart and Ezra looked into my eyes.

I nodded.

My nails dug into his back as he slipped his finger under the fabric.

By the time we got back to our table and took our seats, I realized I never did get the book.

"I'M GOING TO USE MY pass this weekend."

Sofia and I strolled across the quad to class the next morning. After the library, Ezra and I moved to his room to finish the paper and finish we did. We were highly motivated after our adventure in the stacks. We stayed up all night and eventually collapsed fully clothed on his bed two hours before his alarm went off.

"Are you and Zane going to do something?"

The goofy smile on her face said it all. "He wants to take me to dinner for our six-month anniversary. I think he's going to do it, Val. He's going to tell me he loves me."

"Sof, that's great. I'm so happy for you."

"Thanks." She lightly bumped into me. "How lucky are we? I mean, there is still some serious shit going on, but we've got great guys who care about us. It's not just you and me against everyone anymore." She hooked her arm through mine. "Although we do make a great team."

"The best team."

The two of us strode inside and rode the elevator up to the third floor. My eyes landed on the photo the moment we stepped out.

"Whoo! There she is!" Darren darted into my path, blocking the picture. That didn't matter though because he had one of his own. He shoved it in my face. "Will you sign it for me?"

Laughter and catcalls went up around me as what I was seeing penetrated my mind. It was me and Ezra in the library, but you couldn't make out Ezra—only a black-haired boy in a uniform. I, on the other hand, was on full display. My head was tilted back and lips parted mid-moan. What we were doing was obvious from the hand between my legs.

"You piece of shit!" Sofia screeched. She snatched it out of his hands and crumpled it in her fist.

I looked past Darren and saw me... and me... and me again. That photo had been taped to every locker in the hallway.

"What do you think, Valentina?"

My body went rigid. I didn't move or turn my head, but that didn't stop her. The noise from our audience faded as Natalie, Airi, and Isabella lined up in front of me.

Natalie's lips curled into a smirk. "I'm a pretty good photographer, don't you think?"

Rage like I had never felt before consumed me. Pinpricks of sweat broke out on my skin as I trembled. "You... did this?"

"That's right," she sang. "I told you I would get back at you for the tournament." She gestured at her friends. "You can also call it payback for the violin and slashed tires. We know it was you and now *you* know not to mess with the Diamonds again."

"Natalie, you have no idea what you've done." My hands balled into fists. "I'm going to make you regret this."

She scoffed. "Save it, slum trash. No one here is afraid of you. So why don't you stay in your place and I won't have to teach you this lesson again." She cocked her head. "By the way, who is that guy? Or have you been passing it around so much you can't keep track anymore?"

I snapped. I lurched forward, fist reeled back, and then something shot out in front of me.

Natalie's head whipped around with the force of Sofia's punch. She let out a small scream as she spun like a top and collapsed at Airi's feet.

"You crazy bitch!" she shrieked, clutching her jaw.

Sofia towered over her as she shook out her hand. "You messed with the wrong one, Bard. Stay in your place and I won't have to teach you this lesson again."

Airi and Isabella snatched their friend up and dragged her off. The three of them shouted awful things at us as they went, but my attention was solely on Sofia.

I gaped at her. The crowd hanging back to watch us gaped at her. "Sofia Lorraine Richards! What was that?"

"I said we're a team. Natalie went too far. I'll probably punch her again the next time I see her." Sofia smirked. "I told you I wasn't too sweet."

The satisfaction I felt at seeing Natalie go down didn't hang around as we walked down the hall and past those pictures. I wouldn't give my classmates the pleasure of seeing me run around ripping them down, but watching people like Darren feast on a moment between me and Ezra made me sick.

I shuffled into Markham's classroom and made it to my desk with Sofia on my heels.

"They won't get away with this. I promise."

Students filed inside, throwing filthy comments my way. The Diamonds were among the last to walk in. Natalie shot me and Sofia baleful looks as she went past. The only ones who hadn't arrived were the Knights and Markham herself.

Sofia grasped my shoulder. "Evergreen will go mad when he sees what she has done. They—"

Bang!

The entire class jumped as the door flew open. Ryder stalked inside with an expression on his face I knew too well. Behind him, Jaxson, Ezra, and Maverick followed.

I held my breath as Ryder stopped in front of Natalie. The other boys didn't.

Jaxson ripped open the phone box and snatched one out. He put it in Ezra's hand. Ezra didn't hesitate. He reeled back and threw the phone to the floor. It broke in a shower of plastic, metal, and glass as Natalie screamed.

Jaxson took out another one.

"Wait, no!" Airi surged to her feet. "I didn't—"

"Sit down!" Maverick roared. "Now!"

Airi fell back into her seat as Ezra destroyed her phone. He did the same to Isabella's.

Ryder bent until he was inches from Natalie's pale face. "That's done. Now it's time for you to apologize to Valentina."

I could see her shaking from here. "Y-you can't make me."

There was a collective intake of breath. I swallowed as Ryder bared his teeth. "Can't I? You want to test that theory?"

I shivered at his tone. This was the old Ryder... or maybe it wasn't. Maybe this was and will always be him.

"S-she got me first. I was only paying her back for the tournament."

"Valentina didn't get you disqualified, Bard. That was me."

"You? But that's not— Why?!"

"Because I wanted to. So guess how much worse it'll be now that I'm really pissed off. *Apologize*."

It took her a minute. She stared into Ryder's eyes longer than anyone should and must have seen something that changed her mind.

"I'm sorry, Valentina."

"Good." Ryder straightened. "Now I want you and your little friends to take down every single photo and destroy them."

The Diamonds didn't utter a word of protest as they rose and left the classroom. I don't think I ever fully appreciated the Knights and what they did for the school until that moment, but they weren't done.

"I heard you all had a few things to say to Valentina." Ezra moved down one of the rows. "Well, I'm the guy who was with her in the photo so let's hear you say it to me. Go on!" he bellowed.

You could hear a pin drop. No one moved. No one breathed too loudly.

"Say it to me, guys!" Ezra zeroed in on Darren. He got right in the boy's face. "What about you? I know you must have been running your fucking mouth so repeat it to me."

Darren shook his head roughly as he sunk down. His lips were pressed tight.

"No?" Ezra looked around. "No one? Well then, I better not hear another word about it. None of you opens your mouth about that picture or I do to your teeth what I did to those phones. Understood?"

"Yes, Ezra," they chorused.

Markham burst in as they took their seats. "Who is responsible for those photos?! When I find the person who did this—"

"It's been handled, mama," Jaxson cut in. "The Knights took care of it."

Chapter Twelve

I passed the day in a strange mood. No one brought up the photo. They didn't whisper it, mime it—nothing. It was like it never happened.

I hated that people saw me like that, but overpowering that feeling was one I couldn't describe. It overcame me as the Knights unleashed their fury. I could have handled Natalie and the Diamonds on my own, but seeing how much they cared about me had bowled me over.

Somehow I made it through the day and ended up in Markham's class again. My phone vibrated with a notification. I wasn't surprised. I knew this was coming.

Ace: You must feel pretty proud of yourself. You've got the Knights defending your nonexistent honor.

I didn't reply to the text right away. Instead, I opened my camera app and snapped a picture of the box. Then I went back to Ace.

Me: I didn't tell them to do that.

Ace: Nope, but you did hook up with Ezra. That will not happen again.

Me: What does that mean? Why do you care if I hook up with Ezra or any of the Knights? They are all free to date who they want.

Ace: That's where you are wrong. They aren't free. They're mine.

My brows snapped together as I read that final sentence. What the hell?

Me: How are they yours? Is this why you're only targeting me? Because you have some kind of crush on them?

Ace: LOL! A crush? How cute. You think so small, Val, but I expect nothing less from a trashy whore.

I bristled. This asshole was doing everything in their power to make sure I beat them bloody when I finally found out who they were.

Ace: Anyway, you don't need to worry about me right now. What's important here is making sure the message hits home that you're nothing but a slut and not worth their time. So here is what you're going to do: We all fondly remember freshman year when you strutted around the cafeteria in a towel. This time... leave the towel behind.

My eyes widened. *They can't be saying what I think they are.*

Another text came in while I was typing a reply.

Ace: To be clear: strip.

Me: I'm NOT doing that! You're sick!

Ace: Correction: you are doing that.

Me: I'll be kicked out of school!

Ace: That would be a bonus. Think of it this way, you'll end up somewhere a lot worse if I show the police that you covered up a death.

Me: Why are you doing this?! I'm not with Ezra or any of the Knights. I'm not going to date them. You get your wish.

Ace: I'll be sure of that when they see you for the trash you are. Tomorrow. Lunch. If you don't, I send this video to the police.

THE CLASS FADED INTO a dull roar. My textbook sat open in front of me but I couldn't read the words on the page even if I wanted to. My attention was fixed completely on the clock.

The bell that signaled the stroke of noon was a death knell. Slowly, I rose from my seat and left the classroom. My classmates all went one way while I went the other. Into the elevator, down to the first floor, out into the courtyard, and then finally into my building.

My bathrobe awaited me when I stepped into my bedroom. It was tossed haphazardly on the bed from that morning.

I stared unseeingly at it while I pulled my dress over my head. I had thought about what to do all night. I didn't call the Knights. I didn't tell Sofia. This was between me and Ace. They couldn't save me.

I stripped down to my bare skin.

I hated what they had driven me to, but it had to be done. I had no choice. I understood that now.

The wind had picked up by the time I stepped outside. It whipped and played with the hem of my robe so I clutched it tighter. Leaves crunched beneath my bare feet as I crossed the lawn and returned to the main building.

The cafeteria was a riot of noise when I walked inside. No one paid attention to me at first... until I caught Darren's eye.

"Hey, Moon! What the hell are you doing?"

I glared at him. "You'll find out."

Just like that, the room fell quiet as everyone turned to stare at me. I lifted my chin as I kept walking to the dais. I could read the expression of every one of my Knights this time because they were all the same.

Jaxson stood when I placed my foot on the platform. "Val, what are you doing?"

I didn't respond. I skirted around him and climbed onto his chair. Then, I stepped on the table.

All of the Knights were up now.

"Valentina, get down." I felt a hand on my arm but I knocked it off as I reached for the belt of my robe.

"Oh shit," someone shouted. "She's giving us another show!"

The room was quickly awash with catcalls. Guys jumped out of their seats to rush the dais.

"Sit the fuck down!" Ezra roared. He darted in front of the table. "Get out! Everyone out!"

"Come on, Val! Take it off!"

One of the boys tried to grab me again. "Val!"

In one smooth move, I ripped the robe off. The fabric pooled at my feet as the whoops and cheers came to a stuttering halt.

I threw out my hands. "Get a good look!" I cried. "Make sure you get *this* message!"

I wasn't naked. Quite the opposite. I stood above the room in shorts and a plain white t-shirt that I had marked up to tell Ace what I really felt: Fuck You.

I glared into the eyes of everyone who looked my way. "Some piece of shit," I announced, "has been blackmailing me since school started. They thought they would get me to come up here and give you all a striptease, but they forgot who the fuck they were messing with. So listen up, *Ace*, if you're in here. You can do your worst. I can handle it. Just like I'll handle you if I ever find out who you are.

"And one more thing. They're not yours." A smirk spread across my lips. "They're mine."

I got to bask in my glorious moment for another half of a second before Maverick grabbed my arm.

I yelped as I was unceremoniously thrown over his shoulder and carted out of the room.

"Uh, Maverick? I can walk."

He ignored me. The other boys were right behind. I rode his shoulder all the way to the Knight room where he dumped me on the couch.

"Explain," Ryder demanded.

"Gladly." I told them everything. "Ace was pissed that I was with Ezra. They wanted to turn you all off of me for good."

Jaxson came to my side. "Why didn't you tell us?"

"What would you have done? I had two choices: strip or defy them. You couldn't make it for me."

"No," Ezra spoke up. "You're right, we couldn't. But what do we do now? They are going to send the video to the police."

"They might not release it."

"How can you say that?" Ezra asked. "Why wouldn't they?"

"Because you're in it. All of you. They've only focused on me even though we're all in that video. They want to keep us apart but I don't believe they want to hurt you. They said you belong to them."

"They said that because they're insane," Jaxson countered. "We don't know who the hell that is or why they think they own us. We can't predict what they will do."

"What if it's them." Maverick drew my eye. "The Ace of Spades. The Spades believe they own everybody."

I shook my head. "I don't think you have a Spade on your tail. I think you have a stalker."

"A stalker?"

"Yes. Someone followed you into the woods that day and was careful to keep themselves hidden. They won't reveal who they are. They are creepily obsessed with keeping us apart. I don't know what they will do now, but if this is about you, they won't send that video to the police."

"And what about you?" Ryder asked. He moved until he was directly in front of me. "If we have a stalker that is this determined, they will not be happy with what you did today. They could come up behind you and you wouldn't know it was them."

"Then let's do something about that." I got to my feet. "Yesterday, I took a picture of the phone box after I took mine out. The text from Ace was sent ten minutes before I got there. If Ace is a junior, their phone was locked in that box same as all of us, which means they have to be one of the people who took their phone before me. If we match the names to the student numbers; we'll have a list of Ace suspects."

Maverick goggled at me. "Val, that's... brilliant."

I smiled. "Yes, it is, and we can eliminate three people from the jump."

"Airi, Natalie, and Isabella," Ezra spoke up. "I broke their phones and none of them had time to replace them."

"Exactly."

Ryder sprang into action. "Val, get your phone. If Markham puts up a fuss, tell her that it's Knight business. Jaxson, get the list of student numbers. Ezra, get Val some lunch. We're ending this shit now."

WHISPERS FOLLOWED ME the next day. I overheard Ace on the lips of everyone I passed by, but I was watching them as hard as they watched me. We had a list now. We were close to finding Ace. I could feel it.

Jaxson was waiting for me at my locker. There was no hiding now. Not after what I did.

I walked up and boldly kissed him on the lips. "You checking up on me?"

"You mean am I worried about you after you pissed off a psycho? Yes."

"I didn't have a choice." I moved around him and reached for my lock. Arms snaked around my waist.

"I know you didn't and I'm proud of you. No one gets to see that ass but me... and Maverick and Ezra and—"

I playfully bumped him. "I get it," I said as I spun the dial.

"We don't know what they're going to do," he said into my ear. "So I'll be sticking close."

"How close?"

"Very close." His tongue darted out and licked me. "I should probably spend the night with you as well."

"Good idea. Safety first."

We giggled as I threw open my locker. I reached for my chemistry textbook and something caught my eye. Time slowed down. Jaxson's voice faded to a dull roar as I lifted my head and saw it.

Stuck to the top of my locker was a joker card.

"No..." he whispered. The horror in Jaxson's voice didn't scare me as much as his silence. He was speechless.

"Guys, look. She's got the card."

The words were a slap to the face. I sprung forward and ripped it down even though I knew it was too late.

No. No, please. Not again.

"Look at that." Darren's voice grated on my ears. "I guess we're going in for round two. I wonder if you'll survive—"

Jaxson moved so fast he blurred across my vision. One moment Darren was smirking at me and the next he was slammed against the locker.

"You listen up," Jaxson snarled. "There is no round two. You or anyone else touches her; I'll beat you so bad it'll hurt to cry."

Jaxson abruptly released him, letting him fall to the floor. "That goes for all of you! Consider it an order from the Knights! You got that?"

"Yes, Jaxson."

The crowd broke apart, scurrying in every direction as they headed for class. I didn't know what to do. The roaring was getting louder. A band constricted my chest—one I had not felt for a long time.

Eventually, I staggered to class. Jaxson was next to me but nothing he said was going in. It wasn't until halfway through first period when Natalie shot me a triumphant smile that it hit me.

I was marked.

I made it through the rest of my morning classes by a miracle. My friends pounced on me the moment the bell rang for lunch. "You're not going through this again, Val." Sofia's grip on my hand was tight. "If anyone tries to bully you, I'm kicking their ass."

"Seconded."

"Third."

I shot the twins a smile over my shoulder. I think it was a smile anyway. It could have been a grimace. "Thanks, guys, but you should know right now that I'm not letting people hurt you because of me."

"Fuck that," said Kai.

That got another round of agreement.

I sighed. There was nothing I could do if they were determined to tell everyone they had my back, and part of me didn't want to stop them. I could not go through this again.

Silence descended on the lunchroom when I stepped inside. I was really getting tired of that. But something that was different was the Knights all standing when I walked in.

"Listen up," Jaxson bellowed although there was barely a sound. "By now you've heard about the card."

Ezra stepped forward. "We did too and we want to make sure something is very clear."

"Valentina Moon stays," Maverick said. "No one touches her."

Ryder's voice carried through the room. "Because that card is a fake."

"What?!"

That first shout broke the sound barrier and suddenly everyone was yelling. Through it all I didn't look away from the Knights.

What are they doing?

"What do you mean the card is a fake?" Isabella demanded. "How do you know that?"

Ryder turned silver eyes on her. "A real mark is printed on special card stock. The joker is hand-painted and wearing the school colors. This card had none of that. It's a fake most likely put out by the person blackmailing Valentina. They were relying on you idiots to not know the facts and go off at the sight of any joker card."

Isabella flicked her hair over her shoulder. "If that's true, show it to us. Let's see if it's fake."

I saw the moment the light went out behind his eyes. Ryder stepped off the stage and advanced on Isabella. She took the tiniest step back.

"Are you calling me a liar?"

I swear the temperature in the room plunged.

Isabella shook her head. "No, I— I just thought we could make sure this never happens again by showing people what a fake looks like."

"You don't need to know what a fake looks like. You just need to listen to me when I tell you it is."

"Of course, Ryder." She shrank under his gaze. "Sorry."

He looked around at those watching. "Everyone got it?"

A chorus of yeses came back.

It took me a while to pick up my feet and join the lunch line. Was that it? Did the Knights truly end this nightmare before it could begin?

I gazed at them and as the line moved, I felt a rush of such powerful emotion that before I knew it, I was racing up the dais. Maverick stood to catch me as I threw myself in his arms.

"Thank you," I whispered. "Thank you."

His arms were strong, secure, and safe. "I'll never let anyone hurt you again. I—"

"I love you." The words spilled from my lips. I hadn't known they were coming, but they felt right. They felt so right I said it again. "I love you, Maverick."

The others watched us. I had words for them. I was going to tell and show each of them exactly how I felt. No more hiding. No more waiting for the right moment. No more being kept at arm's length.

Ace had tried to take my Knights away from me. I would never let that happen. I would make them mine in every way.

THE ALARM CLOCK JOLTED me awake the next morning. My hand darted out of the covers and smacked the offending thing to the floor.

A laugh filled my ear as Maverick put his arm over my waist. "You can break my clock, but we still have to go to class."

"I don't want to." I twisted around and snuggled into his chest. "You're a Knight. Get me out of classes today."

"I wish I could." He kissed my forehead. "But we've got a paper due."

"Ugh. You're a Knight. Get Coleman fired."

The bed shook with his laugh. "Knights aren't fairy godmothers. I can't fix everything."

"But you did fix one thing for me." I tilted my head back to show him my smile. "We both know that card wasn't a fake. I gambled and lost. Not only is Ace a psychopath and possibly a stalker; they are also a Spade."

He pulled me closer. "I don't care who the fuck they are. We're not playing their game anymore. Getting people to doubt the mark was good, but I don't think it ends here. Whatever happens next; this is war."

Those words banged around in my head as we got dressed and left for homeroom. We walked hand in hand through the quad. I loved being public. Everything would change now.

As we went, my smile faded. I began to notice the looks we were getting.

"What's going on?"

Maverick stopped dead, pulling me up short. "I don't know," he replied as one of the junior girls gave him a wide berth. "But something is up."

We were a few feet away from Markham's class when his phone went off.

"Yeah, Jaxson? What? Slow down. What are you talking about?" My alarm grew as his face went ashen. "But— But that's not possible."

"Maverick, what?" I grabbed his forearms. "What is it?"

Maverick pulled the phone away from his ear. I could still hear Jaxson's voice coming through shouting unintelligibly about something.

"Val, we— We've been marked," he forced out. "The Knights have all been marked."

Unmasked

They are everything to me.

I love Jaxson, Ezra, Maverick, and Ryder the same and in vastly different ways all at once. It's a love that threatens to consume me. To take over every waking second of my final year...

...if only hidden enemies, ancient secret societies, and unsolved murders weren't also competing for my attention.

This will be my hardest term yet.

Not just for the horror of the present, but for the uncertainty of my future. How can I have a life with my knights when someone is determined that I don't survive my senior year at all?

But I will find them. I will expose them.

And by the end... only one will be left standing.

Mailing List

Join my mailing list for info about new releases and treats. No spam ever.

Mailing list: https://www.subscribepage.com/rubyvincent-page

ABOUT THE AUTHOR

Ruby Vincent is a published author with many novels under her belt but now she's taking a fun foray into contemporary romance. She loves saucy heroines, bold alpha males, and weaving a tale where both get their happy ever after.

Made in the USA
Coppell, TX
09 April 2021

53451481R00152